"I don't like you," she mumbled under her breath, so low he could barely make out what she'd said.

"I noticed," he whispered back, in resigned acknowledgement of her feelings toward him.

"Even if you *are* scorching hot and wear sex appeal like a second skin."

Sloan's entire body went stiff. Her breathing was still even and her body hadn't moved away from where she'd spooned with his. Was she awake?

"You think I'm sexy?" he asked, curious as to whether she'd respond and, if so, what she'd say.

"You are so hot you melt my insides just looking at you—but don't think I'll ever tell you that," she answered, her body still relaxed against his. "I won't, because I don't like you."

Asleep. She was talking to him in her sleep. No way would she have just said that and not gone all tense if she were awake.

Sloan grinned. It no longer mattered that Cara didn't like him, because apparently she was as physically aware of him as he was of her. Somehow, at that moment, that seemed a lot more important in the grand scheme of life than merely being liked.

"Good night, Cara," he whispered against her hair, brushing his lips against its silkiness in a soft kiss. "We're going to have this conversation when you're awake, because looking at you melts my insides, too, and I *do* like *you*. I like you way too much."

Dear Reader,

It's funny how real life bleeds over into the imaginary worlds we authors create. Cara and Sloan's story is definitely an example of that. A while back my mentor and dear friend died—the best doctor and one of the greatest men I've ever known—and in this story Cara is dealing with the loss of her father—a man much like my dear friend. Only Cara's father's death has set into play a whirlwind of changes that put Cara's life and heart into a tailspin.

Sloan might be my favourite hero I've ever written… *might* be. He's the kind of man I want for my own daughters some day. A good man with strong morals, a lover of life, and a man who wants to give back to others—a man who loves with all his heart. He's half in love with Cara before he's even met her in person, and can't quite figure out why she, his mentor's daughter, can't stand him.

I had so much fun watching the relationship unfold between these two, as each learns what it means to love someone and to love each other.

As always, I love to hear from my readers. You can reach me at Janice@janicelynn.net or find out what I've been up to via Facebook.

Happy reading!

Janice

NEW YORK DOC TO BLUSHING BRIDE

BY
JANICE LYNN

First published in Great Britain 2015
by Mills & Boon, an imprint of Harlequin (UK) Limited,
Eton House, 18-24 Paradise Road, Richmond, Surrey, TW9 1SR

© 2015 Janice Lynn

ISBN: 978-0-263-25824-0

Harlequin (UK) Limited's policy is to use papers that are natural,
renewable and recyclable products and made from wood grown in
sustainable forests. The logging and manufacturing processes conform
igin.

Janice Lynn has a Masters in Nursing from Vanderbilt University, and works as a nurse practitioner in a family practice. She lives in the southern United States with her husband, their four children, their Jack Russell—appropriately named Trouble—and a lot of unnamed dust bunnies that have moved in since she started her writing career.

To find out more about Janice and her writing visit janicelynn.com.

Books by Janice Lynn

Mills & Boon® Medical Romance™

Flirting with the Doc of Her Dreams
The ER's Newest Dad
NYC Angels: Heiress's Baby Scandal
Challenging the Nurse's Rules
Flirting with the Society Doctor
Doctor's Damsel in Distress
The Nurse Who Saved Christmas
Officer, Gentleman…Surgeon!
Dr Di Angelo's Baby Bombshell

**Visit the author profile page
at millsandboon.co.uk for more titles**

**Janice won The National Readers' Choice Award for
her first book *The Doctor's Pregnancy Bombshell***

To Abby, my daughter, an amazing young woman
whom I hope reaches for the stars without ever
forgetting her inner dreamer. Love you, Baby Girl!

CHAPTER ONE

At first glance, the slim redhead sitting on the funeral chapel's front pew epitomized poise and grace. But as she politely accepted the sympathy being expressed her fingers clenched and unclenched around the crumpled tissue in her hand. Dr. Sloan Trenton would like to hold her hand, let her cling to him to help her get through the next few days, to share the pain they both felt.

No matter how much he felt he knew Dr. Cara Conner, she saw him as a stranger.

Only she wasn't a stranger to him.

From the time Sloan had joined the Bloomberg, Alabama family medicine practice the year before, Preston had enthusiastically talked about his amazing daughter who worked in a downtown Manhattan emergency room. That must be why Sloan had thought of her so much since he had officially met her only yesterday.

He'd stopped by Preston's house to offer his sympathies. His heart had raced like crazy when he'd rung her doorbell, knowing he was finally going to meet her. Despite his exhaustion, his grief over Preston's heart attack, he hadn't been able to stay away. He'd had to go to her, to offer his condolences. He felt as if his own heart had been ripped to shreds at the death of a man who'd treated him as a son. Something Sloan had never had anyone do, blood kin or otherwise.

Probably that was why he felt such a connection to Cara.

Regardless of the reason, he'd been shocked at Preston's daughter's reaction.

She hadn't been out-and-out rude, but she hadn't been receptive to his visit, either, had failed to even invite him into the house and had failed to hide her dislike. He'd stood on Preston's front porch, a house the man had given him a key to, and he'd felt like an awkward inconvenience in Cara's world, like an outsider in a place where he'd, up to that point, finally felt at home.

Maybe it was just grief making her so prickly toward him. After all, she'd just lost her father. Still, his gut instinct warned her reaction ran much deeper than grief over Preston's death.

Sloan swallowed the lump that formed in his throat every time the reality that his mentor and best friend was gone hit him. He moved closer to the brushed steel casket he'd stood vigil by all evening.

Dr. Preston J. Conner had been the best man and doctor Sloan had ever known. He'd been the doctor Sloan aspired to be like. No matter how much he tried, he'd never be half the physician Preston had been.

Just fifteen feet away, Cara stood, wobbling slightly in her black stilettos and slim skirt. Sloan moved forward, determined to catch her if she didn't straighten. Without glancing his way, she headed out of the room, unaware that he couldn't drag his gaze away from her more than a few seconds at a time.

He excused himself from the bank president and a local preacher who had been carrying on a conversation around him and he followed Cara.

Leaving the large old Victorian-style house that had served as one of Bloomberg's two funeral parlors for more than a hundred years, she slipped around to the side garden.

If Sloan followed her, was that outright stalkerish or just the action of a man who was worried about a woman who had just experienced great loss?

He had to at least make sure she was all right.

Hadn't Preston's last words been for him to take care of Cara?

Sloan headed around the side of the building. She was sitting on a bench, looking up at the sky. A pale sliver of moonlight illuminated her just well enough that he could tell she was speaking, but he was too far away to make out what she said or even the sound of her whispered words.

His ribs broke loose and lassoed themselves around his heart, clamping down so tightly that he could barely breathe.

Never had he seen anything more beautiful than the ethereal image she made in the moonlight. Never had he felt such a fascination with a woman.

A commotion behind him had him spinning to see the source, but not before he saw Cara's head jerk toward the noise also, catching him watching her. Great. Now she'd add stalker to whatever other crimes he'd possibly committed.

But he didn't have time to dwell on that. The cause of the noise now had his full attention.

Mrs. Goines, a blue-haired little elderly lady, had fallen while going down the three steps leading out of the funeral parlor. Why she hadn't taken the handicap ramp Sloan could only put down to her stubbornness that she wasn't handicapped or disabled. She had lost her footing and down she'd gone.

He got to the frail little woman almost as quickly as the woman who'd been right behind her—her daughter, if Sloan remembered correctly.

"Mom? Are you okay?" she asked, confirming Sloan's memory of who she was. She leaned over her mother, who moaned in pain.

"I can't move." Ignoring her daughter, Mrs. Goines's gaze connected to Sloan's and she groaned in obvious agony. "I can't get up."

Assessing the position in which she'd fallen and how she'd landed, Sloan winced. She'd landed on her right hip, leg and arm. Her hip and her shoulder had taken the brunt of her weight. He'd seen her in clinic several times since he'd come to Bloomberg. He knew her health history. She was on a biphosphanate medication to strengthen her thin bones, having struggled with osteoporosis for more than a decade. Her weakened bones hadn't been able to withstand the impact of her fall.

"Don't try to move, Mrs. Goines," he ordered in a low, confident tone. "I'm going to check you, but I will need to send you to the hospital for X-rays."

"Is everything okay?" Cara asked, joining them and hunching down next to Sloan. At his dash at the noise, she'd apparently come to investigate. Taking the elderly woman's hand, her expression softened with a compassion that caused Sloan's breath to catch in his throat.

"Mrs. Goines," she chided with a click of her tongue and the twinkle in her eyes that had captured his imagination in Preston's office photos, "were you sliding down the railings again? You know my dad warned you about that."

The woman's pain-filled eyes eased just a tiny bit

with Cara's distracting words. "Remember that, do you, girlie?"

"I remember a lot of things about growing up in this town. Like that you used to sneak me extra peaches when I'd go through school lunch line," Cara told her in a gentle voice. "Can you tell me where you are?"

The woman frowned. "If you don't know, then it should be you being checked by a doctor, not me. It's your father's funeral we're at, girlie."

"You're right," Cara agreed, not explaining that she was checking the woman's neurological status with her question. "Did you hit your head when you fell?"

"If only," Mrs. Goines moaned. "I wouldn't be hurting nearly so much."

"Possibly not, but I'm still glad you didn't hit your head." Cara looked into her eyes, studying her pupils in the glow of the porch and lit walkway. "Can you tell me where you hurt most?"

Completely ignoring Sloan now, Mrs. Goines continued to moan in pain while answering Cara's questions.

Despite the seriousness of the situation, Sloan had to fight a smile at the transformation that had taken place. Gone was the lost, grieving daughter from moments before. In her place was a confident doctor who stepped in and took charge. Truly, she was her father's child.

She moved efficiently and thoroughly, quickly coming to the same conclusion Sloan had while watching her examine the older woman. "She needs X-rays. I'm not sure we will be able to move her. You'll need to call for an ambulance."

He nodded his agreement and motioned to what he held next to his ear. He'd already punched in the emergency dispatcher's number. "I need an ambulance sent to Greenwood's Funeral Parlor," he told the woman who answered the call. "I've a ninety-two-year-old white female who's fallen and can't get up. Probable fractured right hip. Possibly her right humerus, as well."

Cara, Sloan and the crowd that had gathered to see what the commotion was all about stayed with the in-pain Mrs. Goines until the ambulance pulled to a screeching halt in front of the funeral home.

Bud Arnold and his partner Tommy Woodall came up to where Mrs. Goines still lay on the concrete steps at an awkward angle. With her level of pain, moving her had risked further injury so they'd just made her as comfortable as possible where she lay.

"Hey, Dr. Trenton," the paramedics greeted him, then turned to the moaning woman.

"Mrs. Goines, please tell me you didn't try sliding down the handrail," Bud said immediately when he realized who the patient was.

Obviously, there was a story behind Mrs. Goines and handrails. Sloan would get her to tell him about it soon. Maybe when he rounded on her in the morning because no doubt she'd be admitted through the emergency room tonight and he'd check on her prior to Preston's funeral service.

"Hey, Bud," Cara greeted him, causing the man's eyes to bug out with recognition.

"Well, I'll be. If it isn't Cara Conner. Good to see you, pretty girl." Then he recalled why she was in town and his happy greeting turned to solemn remorse. "Sorry to hear about your dad. He was a good, good man. Best doctor I ever knew."

"Thanks, Bud. He was a good man and doctor." She took a deep breath. "Now, let's take care of this good woman lying here in pain. She's going to have to be put on the stretcher. Right hip is broken. I can't be certain if her right shoulder is broken or just shoved out of socket from the impact of her fall. Her right clavicle is fractured, too."

Cara pushed aside the loose material of Mrs. Goines's dress neckline. Sure enough, there was a large bump that had fortunately not broken through the skin but which did indicate that the woman's collarbone had snapped from the impact against the concrete steps.

"I do believe you're right, Doc," Bud agreed. "Let's get this feisty little lady to the emergency room."

The two paramedics lowered the stretcher as far as it would go and positioned Mrs. Goines to where they could slide her onto the bedding.

Cara and Sloan both positioned themselves where they wouldn't interfere with Bud and Tommy's work but where they could help stabilize Mrs. Goines's body as much as possible during the transfer.

"On the count of three, we're going to lift you onto the stretcher," Bud told their patient.

Although Mrs. Goines cried out in pain, the transfer went smoothly.

Sloan turned to Cara and smiled. "You should move back to Bloomberg. We make a good team, you and I."

Her gaze narrowed as if he'd said something vulgar. "You and I are not a team," she said, low enough that only he could hear. "And I will never move back to Bloomberg."

She stood, bent and said something to Mrs. Goines, who was now strapped onto the stretcher to prevent her from falling off while they rolled her to where the ambulance waited. Then she nodded toward Bud and Tommy and disappeared inside the funeral home.

Slowly, Sloan rose to his feet, scratched his head and

wondered what he'd ever done to upset Preston's daughter so completely and totally.

And why he'd never wanted a woman to like him more.

People Cara had known her entire life shook her hand, hugged her and pressed sloppy kisses to her cheek. People told her how wonderful her father had been, what a difference he'd made in their lives, stories of how he'd gone above and beyond the call of duty time and again during his thirty-plus years of practicing medicine in Bloomberg—as if Cara didn't know firsthand what he'd sacrificed for his patients.

She knew. Oh, how she knew.

Everyone milled around, talking to each other, saying what a shame it was the town had lost such a prominent and beloved member. All their words, their faces churned in Cara's grieving mind, a whirlwind of emotional daggers that sliced at her very being.

Her gaze went to the one stranger in their midst. A stranger only to her, it seemed as he was the other person receiving condolences from everyone in the funeral parlor.

Acid gurgled in her stomach, threatening to gnaw a hole right through her knotted belly.

Why was *he* getting handshakes, hugs and sloppy kisses from people like little old arthritic Mary Jo Jones and Catherine Lester? Why did everyone treat him as if he'd suffered just as great a loss as she had?

Preston had been her father, her family. Not his.

Sloan Trenton was an outsider. Someone her father had recruited to join his practice about a year ago when he'd apparently given up on her joining any time in the near future. Then again, maybe not an outsider. How many times had her father said Sloan was like the son he'd never had? How impressed he was by the talented doctor he'd added to his practice? Every time they'd talked, he'd been "Sloan this" and "Sloan that."

So perhaps the bitterness she felt didn't really stem from Sloan being treated as if his grief was as great as her own. Perhaps her bitterness had started long ago while listening to her father go on and on about the man, about how Sloan loved Bloomberg and its people almost as much as Preston himself did, about how Sloan tirelessly gave of himself to the town, that watching Sloan was like a flashback to himself thirty years before, except that he'd been married. Of course, her father had joked, Bloomberg's most eligible bachelor wasn't still single because of a lack of trying on many a female's part.

Sloan. Sloan. Sloan. Gag. Gag. Gag.

Dr. Sloan Trenton could do no wrong in her father's eyes and, deep down, Cara resented that. Although he'd loved her, she had never achieved that complete admiration because she'd had too much of her mother's love of the big city in her blood, too much of her mother's resentment of how much Bloomberg stole from their lives, and her father couldn't, or wouldn't, understand.

She'd had enough of her father in her to love medicine, but she hadn't been willing to have her life light snuffed out by the demanding town that had taken its toll on her family. Give her the anonymity of the big-city emergency room any day of the week.

She huffed out an exasperated breath.

The tall, lean object of her animosity couldn't have heard her sigh, not over the chatter in the crowded funeral home and the distance that separated them, but Sloan turned as if she had called out his name. Filled with concern, his coppery brown gaze connected to hers and held, despite the men still talking to him as if he was focused solely on them.

She narrowed her eyes in dislike, not caring what he thought of her, not caring about anything except the gaping crater in her broken heart. She focused all her negative energy toward him, as if he were somehow to blame for her loss, as if he could have prevented her father from dying. Logically, she knew he couldn't have.

Sloan's handsome features drew tight. He looked almost as exhausted as she felt. But she didn't like him, didn't want him there. Everything about him disturbed her.

Had from the moment she'd opened the door to find him standing on her front porch yesterday during the midst of her major boo-hoo fest. She'd have hated anyone to see her that way, but she especially hated that her father's beloved prodigy had witnessed her meltdown.

Currently, one of his coal-dark brows arched in acknowledgement of her enmity, no doubt questioning her dislike. Why not? Obviously, he was well loved within the community. Her father had sure loved him. The townspeople loved him. With his inky black hair, those amazing eyes, handsome face and a body that, despite her doom-and-gloom mental state, she had to admit belonged on a television hunk rather than a small-town doctor, women loved him. Why would he expect anything less than adoration from her?

"Oh, Cara, your dad is going to be so missed at the hospital," Julie Lewis, Cara's closest friend during grade school, sympathized, plopping down next to her on the long wooden front pew and wrapping her in a tight hug.

Cara leaned her head on her longtime friend's shoulder,

grateful for the excuse to break eye contact with Sloan.
Julie's light, flowery perfume filled Cara's nostrils with
memories of when they'd first started wearing makeup
and perfume. Her friend still wore the same honeysuckle
scent as she'd worn throughout high school.

"I can't imagine not hearing his booming voice in the
hospital hallways," Julie continued, shaking her head
in slow denial, her long brunette curls tickling the side
of Cara's face.

Cara remembered reading something online about
Julie working in the hospital lab as a phlebotomist.

"This town has truly lost one of its greatest."

"Truly," Cara agreed, soaking in the remembered
warmth of her childhood friend. She'd grown up with
this woman and yet these days Julie was a virtual
stranger. Other than the occasional message or post
on social media, she'd pretty much lost touch with her
Bloomberg friends years ago during medical school.
She'd been so crazy busy, making sure she distanced
herself from everything Bloomberg, making sure she'd
aced everything she'd done so as not to disappoint her
father.

Only she'd been the biggest disappointment of all
when she'd opted not to return to Bloomberg to practice.

He'd just not understood her love of the big city and
the excitement that flowed through her veins at working
in emergency medicine in the Big Apple. Then again,
he'd never understood her mother's broken heart at leaving the big city, either. Cara only did from having spent
many hours reading her mother's diaries. She'd clung
to those handwritten pages of her mother pouring her
heart out as a link to a woman she mostly remembered
from photos.

"Poor Sloan." Her friend's attention turned to the

man standing near her father's casket. He'd been there all evening. "He's taken this so hard."

Cara's lips pursed. Of course he had. Because he was the son her father had never had. Ugh. She really didn't like the bitterness flowing through her. Anyone who knew her would say she was a positive person, a regular little Miss Sunshine most of the time. But her disposition toward Sloan could only be described as thunderous.

"He idolized Preston."

"No doubt," Cara agreed, in as neutral a voice as she could muster. No one need know of her dislike of Sloan. She wouldn't be here but a few days, then she'd leave Bloomberg forever. Let Sloan give himself to the townspeople to the sacrifice of all else in his life. Cara could give all those matchmakers a hundred and one reasons why they should keep looking elsewhere. A man as devoted to this town as her father had been was admirable but didn't bode well for his wife and kids.

"Rex said Sloan wouldn't leave Preston, that he rode in the ambulance to the hospital, worked alongside the paramedics, stayed in the hospital with him long after he'd been pronounced." Her gaze softened as she looked at the handsome but tired-appearing man being hugged by yet another little old lady. "Poor, poor Sloan," Julie sympathized.

Guilt hit Cara. The man had been there for her father, had tried to resuscitate him, had apparently gotten a heartbeat restarted with CPR, but his damaged heart hadn't been able to sustain a rhythm.

No doubt the stress of the past few days was taking its toll and that's why she felt such irritation toward a man who was obviously a paragon of the community and whom her father had loved. Shame on her.

She didn't usually dislike someone so thoroughly and intensely. Actually, she didn't usually dislike someone, period. That was an honor Sloan Trenton held all on his own.

"He coaches Rex Junior's little-league team, you know."

No, Cara hadn't known.

"And is an assistant pack leader with the Tiger Cubs."

Gee, did he also wear a red cape and tights with a big *S* on the chest? Not that he wouldn't look good in tights. She might not like him but she wasn't blind to the man's physical attributes. Which perhaps made her dislike him all the more. Why couldn't he at least have been ordinary rather than having those amazing coppery eyes and a smile that would leave most Hollywood beaus green with envy?

CHAPTER TWO

"THAT'S WONDERFUL," CARA said to her friend, instead of expressing her immediate thought. Just a few days then she'd never have to think of Super Sloan Trenton or this town again. She'd make her mother proud.

"Yes, he is." Julie elbowed her, causing Cara to scoot a little on the pew. "Some lucky, smart woman is going to have herself a treasure when she lands that man."

Cara's eyes widened. Surely her friend wasn't hinting…not at her father's funeral visitation…not when she knew Cara would never get serious with a mini-me of her father? But when she met her friend's gaze, Julie nodded and grinned from ear to ear.

"He's a good man, Cara." Julie eyed him as if he were Mr. Perfection. "A woman could do a lot worse than coming home to Sloan every night. Just look at him. I love my Rex, but men don't come any hotter than that one."

Any moment Cara expected Julie to fan her face.

Then she did.

Cara resisted an eye roll. Barely.

"As hard as it is to believe, his insides are even better than that yummy exterior. The man has a heart of gold."

"I have a boyfriend, you know." Not to mention that Julie had a husband and child and shouldn't be calling another man yummy and looking at him as if he were chocolate-dipped, right?

"That fancy trauma surgeon you've been dating since your residency? I've seen the pictures of you two and your travels online." Julie gave a low whistle. "He's a looker all right, but something is missing there. He's a little plastic, don't you think?"

Plastic? Not hardly.

"John is a wonderful man." Nothing was missing between her and John. She planned to marry him. Their relationship was wonderful. Wasn't that what she'd told her father repeatedly? What she told herself repeatedly?

"Wonderful is okay." Julie wasn't going to be swayed. "But Sloan is the total package. I'm pretty sure your father handpicked him for you to come home to."

Julie thought... Was that why her father...? No, she'd been with John years before her father had recruited Sloan. He'd liked John. He'd told her he did.

Had the words come from someone other than her father, she might have thought they'd been said only for her benefit. Preston hadn't been known for holding back his true thoughts. He'd have told her if he hadn't approved of the brilliant trauma surgeon she'd taken a liking to when she'd been in residency.

Her father hadn't picked Sloan for her because she'd already picked the man she'd be sharing her future with. She'd told Preston as much, that when John asked her to marry him, she planned to say yes.

That had been last month when her father had flown to New York for a medical conference and spent a few days with her. Of course, John hadn't asked her yet and had been acting a little weird lately, but that was probably only due to how busy his hospital schedule had been the past few months.

"Besides, where is this boyfriend? He should be here with you," Julie pointed out in a tone unflattering to John. Her lips pursed with disapproval. "A man should be with his woman at her father's funeral. No excuses."

"He's a trauma surgeon. He can't just walk away from his job at the drop of a hat. Not unless it was an emergency. There was nothing John could do to help." Or so he'd bluntly told her when she'd mentioned him coming with her. Logically, even if his crassness had hurt, he'd been right. She hadn't pushed for him to drop everything to come with her. But she'd wanted him to do just that, even though, goodness knew, the emergency room would be crazy enough with her unexpectedly gone, much less her and one of the trauma surgeons.

But they would have gotten by... No, she wasn't going to let those thoughts in. John would be here if there had been anything he could do. She couldn't blame him for not wanting to spend time in Bloomberg when he didn't absolutely have to. He loved city life even more than she did.

"Yeah," Julie tsked. "Nothing he could do, except hold your hand, comfort you and keep you from being alone during your father's funeral."

Well, there was that.

Cara didn't want to be having this conversation. Not right now. Not ever. Because as much as she told herself she understood, she also acknowledged that she would have gone with John had their roles been reversed. That he hadn't even considered it hurt more than a smidge.

Ready to end their conversation, Cara managed a tight smile toward her friend and was grateful to see another familiar face waiting to give her sympathy. "Um,

okay, I'll keep that in mind, Julie. Thanks for your condolences. Good to see you."

"You do that, and, yes, Cara, it's so good to see you
home, but I hate that it's under these circumstances."
Her friend squeezed her tightly, filling Cara's nostrils
yet again with honeysuckle and another wave of memories. "Your dad will be missed by everyone in Bloomberg. For that matter, so are you."

She chose to ignore Julie's mention of her being
missed. Yes, her father would be missed by Bloomberg,
but even more so by his daughter. She may not live in
Bloomberg, but she did talk to her father several times
a week. Usually their conversations had consisted of
what new restaurant or show she had gone to that week
or she'd recount some odd case that had come into the
emergency room. On her father's end, he'd talked about
Bloomberg and Sloan.

She'd gotten to where she'd dreaded their next Sloan
the Wonder Boy session. Now, she'd listen to her father
read the phone book just to hear his voice.

A fresh wave of moisture stung Cara's eyes and she
squeezed them shut. She would make it through the next
couple of days and then truly leave Bloomberg, better
known to her as Gloomberg, the name she'd given the
town during high school.

Eventually, the funeral-home crowd began to thin.

Thank God. Sloan felt exhausted. As if being at Preston's visitation wasn't trying enough, Mrs. Goines's fall
and Cara's words had zapped what little adrenaline he'd
still been operating on.

As the last visitor, who'd just finished talking with
Cara, gave their condolences to Sloan, the funeral director came to him to clarify the next day's arrangements.

"I'll check with Cara to see what she prefers," he told Irving Greenwood, the pudgy, balding third-generation funeral-home director. The Greenwood's Funeral Parlor had been serving Bloomberg for more than a hundred years. Lots of Bloomberg's businesses could boast such a rich heritage. That deep sense of family and belonging was what had drawn Sloan to Bloomberg.

That and Dr. Preston Conner.

Bracing himself for whatever Cara threw at him, Sloan's heart picked up pace. Every breath he took sounded loud, forced as he crossed the room to where she sat, hands in her lap, eyes cast downward. She looked lost, alone, elegantly fragile.

Her emotions were everywhere. Understandably so. After all, she'd lost her father unexpectedly. No wonder she was upset. Although he seemed to be the only target of her negative emotions.

"Hey." Sloan gently called her attention to where he stood in front of her. He wasn't sure if she'd been lost in her own thoughts or if she'd purposely been ignoring him. "Mr. Greenwood asked how you wanted the flowers and such handled. I told him I would discuss the matter with you and let him know."

Complexion pale, she blinked up at him as if she'd forgotten he existed, as if their encounter with Mrs. Goines had never happened. "I don't understand. What about the flowers?"

He motioned to the room that could currently have doubled as a florist shop. "They're all yours. Do you want everything not left at the graveside delivered to Preston's house tomorrow afternoon?"

She glanced around at the room that overflowed with flowers, ceramic statues, blankets, bibles and other sympathy mementos. Her expression became confused. "Please, no. What would I do with them?"

Good question. What did a person do with flower arrangements and such following a funeral? Sloan had no idea. He'd never known his parents, had grown up in foster-homes and had certainly never experienced a funeral from this perspective. "I could help you go through everything. There might be a few items you want to keep. We could take the live flowers to the nursing home or hospital, distribute them amongst the patients and staff there, and hopefully add a smile to their day." He smiled, hoping Cara would do the same, even if only a small curving of her lips.

She didn't.

Obviously considering what he'd suggested, she toyed with her bottom lip. "There's nothing I want to keep. It could just all be delivered there to begin with and we wouldn't have to go through anything. Give them to Dad's nursing-home patients, the nurses or whomever you think best. All I ask is that a running list of items and who gave them be kept so I can send appropriate thank-you notes."

Her expression pinched and she rubbed her temple. "Or does the funeral home do that? I've no idea." Fatigue etched on her lovely face, she ran her gaze over the abundance of tokens sent in Preston's memory. "I'd asked that everyone make a donation to the local heart association rather than send flowers. That would have been much easier to deal with, really."

Sloan would have liked to have sat down next to her in the pew. He felt ridiculous towering above her. Despite her momentary politeness, she wouldn't welcome him sitting next to her. He didn't need a genius

IQ to figure that one out. Still, he attempted an empathetic smile.

"I'm sure lots of donations have been made, too. The town's people want to show their love and appreciation for all that your father has done for them over the years. No one has given so much of himself for the benefit of others as your father did for Bloomberg."

She nodded absently, glanced around the room, now empty except for them and the coffin. Her face paled to a pasty white and her knuckles threatened to burst through the thin layer of skin covering them. A sob almost broke free from her pale lips. She managed to stop it, but not before Sloan realized what she'd done. His heart squeezed in a painful vise-like grip.

"Are you okay?" That was a stupid question. Of course she wasn't okay. She'd bury her father in less than twenty-four hours.

But rather than blast him for his ridiculous question, as he'd expected and braced himself for, she just shook her head. "No. I need to get out of here. Please. Just get me out of here."

He wasn't sure what she intended him to do, and there wasn't much he wouldn't do to ease the strain on her face. When she didn't move, he reached for her hand. "Let me help you."

Still looking drained and a bit panicky, she put her hand in his.

Several things registered all at once. Her hand sent chills through his entire body, probably from their sheer frigidness, although he couldn't be sure because there was something electric in the feel of her skin against his, too. Second, she shook. Again, this could be from how cold her hands were but he suspected it had more to do with the situation. Another was how fragile she felt in his grasp. Preston's daughter was a strong, independent woman, a bit of a daredevil and a phenomenal athlete. At the moment, she wasn't any of those things. She was a little girl who'd just lost her father and she looked overwhelmed.

Without a word, Sloan led her to his Jeep, helped her into the passenger seat. She had a rental car at the funeral home, but she didn't need to be driving. Not with the way she was shaking, with how utterly exhausted she appeared. He hadn't slept much the past few days either, between covering his and Preston's patients and his own grief. But at the moment he was the stronger of Cara and himself.

"Sorry I don't have the top on." He rarely kept the top on the Jeep because he liked the freedom of the air whipping about him. "It'll be a bit windy."

"Thank you," she murmured, barely loud enough for him to make out her words. "My mind just wanted to get out of there, but my body didn't seem to know how to leave. Or maybe it was my heart that didn't want to go."

"A normal stress reaction."

"I'm not stressed," she automatically argued, her shoulders stiff.

"Okay, you're not stressed," he agreed, not willing to debate with her since they both knew the truth. He started the Jeep and pulled out of the funeral parlor parking lot, heading down the highway toward the quiet neighborhood where Preston's house was located.

About halfway to Maple Street he glanced toward where she sat, staring blankly out the open doorway. The wind tugged at her hair, pulling strands free from where she had it pinned back. Utter fatigue was etched on her face. He reached across the seat, put his hand over hers. That skin-to-skin electricity zapped him again.

Her head jerked toward him. Had she felt it, too?

Regardless, she looked ready to demand he take her back to Greenwood's, that she'd only temporarily lost her mind in asking for his help. But whatever had sparked to life within her deflated just as quickly. Without a word, she went back to staring out the open doorway. Within seconds her body relaxed and her head slumped against the headrest.

Hand still tucked beneath his, she'd gone to sleep.

He parked the car in front of Preston's gray-and-white Victorian-style home, jumped out and went to Cara's side of the car.

Should he wake her or just carry her inside?

No doubt she'd not slept much, if at all, the night before. If he woke her, would she be able to go back to sleep or would she lie grieving through the long night hours?

Memories of her tearstained face from the day before decided it for him.

Digging his key ring out of his pocket, he unlocked the front door, went back to the Jeep and carefully scooped Cara into his arms.

She was as light as a feather.

And smelled of heaven.

Or as close to heaven as Sloan had ever smelled. Like the soft, sweet fragrance of cherry candy mixed with an amazing, almost addictive freshness that made him want to inhale deeply. Then there were those electric zings. His entire body sparked with excitement.

He held a woman who had fascinated him for months, long before he'd met her. As he'd dated and tried to make a life for himself in Bloomberg, he'd found himself comparing every woman to the woman Preston often spoke of, never satisfied, always feeling as if he was waiting for something more.

Waiting for her to come home perhaps?

Which made no sense.

He blamed Preston. Preston compared every woman Sloan dated to Cara so, of course, Sloan had done the same. The man's dying words had been a request for Sloan to promise to take care of Cara.

A promise Sloan had given and meant.

But, much as he didn't understand his interest in Cara, he couldn't blame everything on Preston. Cara herself had captured his imagination with the various photos of her hanging on Preston's office wall.

Sloan did his best to tamp down the awareness of her that his body couldn't seem to prevent because he was positive that his all-too-male response wasn't what his friend had meant regarding taking care of his daughter. Besides, she was exhausted, grieving for her father. He had no right to be thinking of her as a desirable woman, to be aware of her feminine attributes. He should only be seeing her as the grieving daughter of a man he'd loved.

He kept telling himself that as he carried her into her room, managed to get the covers pulled back, and gently placed her in her bed.

The glow from the hallway light illuminated her lovely face, free from anguish for the first time since he'd met her, with the exception of when she'd been caring for Mrs. Goines. Then her natural nurturing instinct had taken over. He ached to see the twinkle in her eyes that shone in Preston's photos, to hear laughter spill from her full lips, to have her look at him with something other than disdain.

Unable to resist, he brushed a strand of hair away

from her face, stroking his finger over the silky smoothness of her skin.

Based upon her reaction to meeting him, he doubted he'd ever experience any of the things he'd like to experience about Cara, which was a real shame because she fascinated him. Probably because of his love of Preston. Probably.

If only he could convince himself of that.

He turned to leave but her hand grabbed his.

"Don't go."

Sloan stood perfectly still. Was she even awake or just reaching out in her sleep? He turned, met her sleepy gaze. "Cara?"

"I don't want to be alone in this lonely house. Not tonight." Her voice was small, almost childlike in its plea. "Please, don't go."

Sloan knew staying shouldn't be an option. Not in Bloomberg. His Jeep was parked outside. Everyone knew his Jeep. Bloomberg was a small town. Nothing would happen. Not when she was so distraught, but, still, the right thing for him to do would be to leave, to not give gossips anything to gnaw upon.

But walking away from her might take a much stronger man than he'd ever claimed to be.

CHAPTER THREE

CARA CLUNG TO Sloan's hand as if letting go would mean falling into an abyss she might never climb back out of.

She just might.

Goose bumps covered her skin. Her insides trembled. Her teeth fought chattering.

Which was crazy. The house wasn't cold. Not really.

But she felt chilled all the way to her bones, had from the moment she'd lost contact with Sloan's body heat when he'd laid her into her childhood bed. She'd suddenly felt more alone than she could recall ever feeling.

In his arms, and in the cocoon of her exhaustion, she'd felt warm, safe, not alone.

She'd not slept the night before, had tried, but the house haunted her, filling her mind with noises and memories of days gone past.

By the time she'd left for the funeral she'd been grateful for a reason to leave the ghostly haven.

She shivered again and grasped Sloan's hand tighter as she felt his inner struggle on whether to go or stay. No wonder. She didn't like him, hadn't been receptive to any of his friendly overtures. Yet now she was begging him to stay as if he was the only thing protecting her from nighttime monsters.

He was.

"Don't go," she pleaded, grateful for the dim lights. She hated begging. She hated the thought of being alone in this house even more. "I need you."

Still he wavered. "Are you sure, Cara? I don't want to take advantage of you."

Please. She rolled her eyes. Typical man. She just wanted him to ward off the ensuing nightmares and he thought she was offering sex.

Perhaps she couldn't fault him for that because maybe her pleas had sounded as if she wanted more than what she'd meant.

"So long as you keep your clothes on, Casanova, and I keep on my clothes, you aren't taking advantage. I just don't want to be alone. Please, don't make me."

The dark shadows of the room didn't hide him digesting her words. His expression confused, he looked down at where she held his hand. "Just so we're clear, what is it you want from me, Cara?"

Her brain felt fuzzy and she almost said, "Everything." But that was all wrong. All she wanted from him was the comfort of knowing another person was near, that she wasn't really alone in this house, in the world. She needed human contact. Not *him* really. Just another human near to offer companionship, to ground her to reality.

"Just hold me and don't let me go."

He still looked torn. She wished she could read his mind to know his thoughts. But then his lips pursed and he gave one slight nod.

"I can do that."

His answer seemed odd, but perhaps that was her fuzzy, fatigue and grief-laden brain talking. "I never thought you couldn't."

A small smile tugged at one corner of his lips. "I suspect you have a sharp tongue, Cara."

If Cara weren't so cold, feeling so emotionally bereft, if her eyelids weren't so heavy, she might have smiled at his comment. Wasn't that what her father had often said of her mother? That she'd had a tongue so sharp she could cut diamonds with a few well-chosen words? Odd. She hadn't thought of that in years. Instead of acknowledging the memories flooding her, she wrapped her arms around herself and shivered again. "I'm so cold."

Sloan sucked in a deep breath and crawled into the bed beside her, pulling her into his arms and cradling her next to his long, lean, warm body. "You won't be for long, Cara. I promise."

She wasn't.

Instead, she closed her eyes and, although being in bed with him should have kept her wide-awake, she slept, peaceful in the knowledge that he was there.

Not only there but stroking her hair, telling her how sorry he was at her loss, at how her father had been a good man and would be sorely missed. His low, gentle voice soothed aches deep inside her. She snuggled closer into him, knowing that if she wakened and needed him, he would still be there for the simple reason that he'd said he would be.

Funny how much that thought comforted her when he was essentially a stranger and she didn't like him.

Still, her father had liked him, trusted him, which was partially the problem. But in a moment of crisis that had to count for something.

In his arms was the only place she'd found any comfort since her entire world had turned upside down with a phone call he'd been the one to make.

* * *

Sloan lay very still, listening to the even sounds of Cara breathing. She'd gone right back to sleep. That was probably a good thing because no matter how many times he reminded his mind that this was a good deed, his body responded to her closeness in an all-male way.

He inhaled a slow whiff of the scent of her hair. Clean with a soft cherry flavor. That's what she smelled like. Cherry blossoms.

Unable to resist, he ran his fingers into her hair, stroking the sweet softness of her tresses between his fingers.

What was he doing?

Sighing, he let go of her hair and wrapped his arm back around her body, holding her close.

She wriggled against him, causing torturous awareness to zing to life.

"I don't like you," she mumbled under her breath, so low he barely could make out what she said.

"I noticed," he whispered back in resigned acknowledgement of her feelings toward him.

"Even if you are scorching hot and wear sex appeal like a second skin."

Sloan's entire body went stiff. Her breathing was still even and her body hadn't moved away from where she spooned with his. Was she awake?

"You think I'm sexy?" he asked, curious as to whether she'd respond and, if so, what she'd say.

"You are so hot you melt my insides just looking at you—but don't think I'll ever tell you that," she answered, her body still relaxed against his. "I won't, because I don't like you."

Asleep. She was talking to him in her sleep. No way

would she have just said that and not gone all tense if she were awake.

Despite his current uncomfortable predicament, Sloan grinned. It no longer mattered that Cara didn't like him, because apparently she was as physically aware of him as he was her. Somehow, at the moment, that seemed a lot more important in the grand scheme of life than merely being liked.

"Good night, Cara," he whispered against her hair, brushing his lips against the silkiness in a soft kiss. "We have a long day ahead of us tomorrow but we'll get through it. Then we're going to have this conversation when you're awake and not mentally and emotionally exhausted, because looking at you melts my insides, too, and I do like you. I like you way too much."

Cara gradually became aware of her surroundings, drifting somewhere between sleep and an awareness of the world around her. The quietness was the first thing that struck her. No New York City noises in the background of her inner world, as she'd expected.

But her sleepy inner world definitely had noises.

Male noises.

Soft male breath sounds.

And warmth. She felt so absolutely warm that she hated to move and risk letting any coldness seep into her snuggly world.

John didn't usually hold her like this. He wasn't a snuggler and said he couldn't breathe if she was in his personal space, that she made him sweat. Cara slept on her side of the bed and John slept on his. They met in the middle from time to time, but lately that had been less and less frequently.

Actually, Cara couldn't recall the last time she and

John had had sex or held each other. Way before her
father's last visit.

She couldn't recall the last time he'd smelled so won-
derfully manly, either. A light spicy musk that made her
want to remember sex, to remember intimacy, that made
her want to wiggle her body against his, and to have
him want her, not just want her, but have to have her.

Which she must have done, because his arm tightened around her and his lower half woke up. Way up.

Good. Since her father's visit she'd gone from thinking John was going to propose to wondering if he even
wanted her anymore. Maybe she hadn't wanted to admit
it to herself or to anyone else, but something had definitely changed in their relationship. These days he certainly didn't seem to care one way or the other if they
maintained a physical relationship.

Sex wasn't the most important aspect of a relationship to Cara, but the closeness of being intimate with
one's mate was important. Very important, and she
missed that intimacy.

She missed being held and touched and loved.

Which was silly. Of course John loved her. He told
her every morning and every night just like clockwork.
Just as she told him.

She was being held and touched and loved right now
in an *mmmm, good* kind of way and she craved the feelings rushing through her more than she'd realized or
been willing to admit.

His lips brushed against her hair in a caress that
could only be described as worshipful. She rolled over,
wanting to feel them against her mouth, to have him kiss
her, to make love to her with this newfound passion.

He must have been waiting for her, because he
immediately covered her mouth with his. His lips toyed
masterfully with hers, teasing, tasting, tantalizing.

Mmmm, she thought. So good. She didn't recall John kissing so well, or with so much passion, but she wasn't complaining. All her insides were coming alive at how he was kissing her so enthusiastically, at how his body moved against hers, making her all too aware of the clothes separating their bodies. She arched into him, ran her hands into his hair, held him close, kissed him back with an enthusiasm that matched his own, awed at the butterflies dancing in her belly. Lower. It had been so long since she'd felt this way, since she'd wanted, felt wanted, desirable, needed. Had she ever?

"Cara," he moaned. "You feel so good."

Only "he" hadn't been the he she was expecting. He wasn't John and all the feelings hastening through her came to a quick halt.

No longer sleepy, Cara's eyes sprang open and her body jerked away from the man in her bed.

In horror, everything came rushing back.

The awful phone call she'd gotten, telling her that her father had died.

Making arrangements at work to be off for her father's funeral.

John refusing to go with her.

Flying to Pensacola, renting a car, then driving across the Florida-Alabama state line to Bloomberg.

The bittersweetness of walking into her childhood home and it being empty of the man she associated with everything about the place.

Sitting at the funeral home, longing to be anywhere else but in Gloomberg.

Her fatigue, fear and utter loss.

Her begging a man she didn't like to spend the night in her bed because she hadn't wanted to be alone.

Oh, yeah, everything came rushing back in vivid color. No doubt her cheeks glowed in vivid color, as well.

"Good morning," Sloan greeted her sheepishly, raking his fingers through his dark hair and smiling at her as if waking up in each other's arms was no big deal. As if the kisses they'd just shared had been no big deal.

She didn't do that. John was her one and only and they'd been together years. She was going to marry him, for goodness' sake!

"What are you doing?" She ignored his greeting and how absolutely gorgeous he looked first thing in the morning with his tousled black hair and thickly fringed coppery-brown eyes. She went on the attack. Much better to be on the offensive than to have to defend her weakness, to have to explain those kisses. How could she explain what she didn't understand? "I asked you to hold me, not molest me."

The light in his molten eyes morphed into dark confusion. "Molest you?"

Not giving heed to the guilt that hit her, she pushed against his chest, needing him out of her bed, out of her room, her house, her life. She couldn't breathe. She needed him gone. He epitomized everything wrong in her life. "It's time for you to leave."

"Stay. Leave. You're a bossy woman, Cara Conner. Then again, I'd heard that about you more than once. That you're a leader, not a follower." He was trying to make light of their situation, to defuse what had just happened between them. Under different circumstances, Cara might have appreciated his teasing, but she felt too raw to let go of the panic inside her. She'd been kissing him, a virtual stranger. She'd enjoyed kissing him! That had to be because of her crazy emotional state over losing her only living relative. Had to be.

"Don't act as if you know me. You don't." His words were her father's. She knew that. But these were horrible times. The worst of times. Times of which he'd been the bad-news bearer. She'd made them shoddier by inviting a man she didn't know to spend the night in her childhood bed. Shame on her.

They were both still dressed and nothing physical had happened, not really, because that kiss and body grinding so didn't mean anything. She felt emotionally violated all the same, as if something had passed between them during the long night hours when he'd held her, keeping her body safely tucked next to his and protecting her from whatever demons she'd feared. No one had ever held her that way. Not her father. Certainly not John.

That didn't mean she suddenly liked Sloan.

To prove it to herself, she narrowed her gaze and practically growled at him.

"You are obviously not a morning person." Sloan sat up on the side of the bed, raked his fingers through his hair again and shook his head. "For the record, you were the one doing the molesting just then. I was just an innocent victim of your early-morning assault and rather fervent kisses."

Cara's face flamed.

"Not that I'm complaining, because I'm not. I quite enjoyed what just happened between us. But I won't take blame for something I didn't do," he continued, looking way too handsome to have just woken up. "Not even from someone who looks as beautiful as you."

Flattery would get him nowhere. "Innocent victim, my—"

"Shame. Shame," he interrupted, wagging his finger at her. "Watch your language. Preston still has his curse-word jar on the kitchen counter. Would hate for you to have to make a donation first thing out of bed."

Immediately, all the oxygen left the room.

Or maybe it was just Cara's lungs that had become deprived, because Sloan seemed to be breathing just fine.

How dared he remind her of her father's curse-word jar?

What right did he have to tell her about her father's habits? Did he think she didn't know? That just because she'd chosen to live her life where she wanted rather than where he wanted her to be made her love her father less somehow? That her location made her forget growing up in this house and her father's habits? Hardly. She remembered all too well.

Her anger toward Sloan grew tenfold.

"Get out of here," she ordered, focusing all her hurt and frustrations toward him and wondering at how the cold blast didn't slam him out of her bed and against the wall like a splattered bug against a windshield. "Now, before I call the law and have you forcibly removed."

Looking way too calm for someone under attack, Sloan glanced at the wristwatch he still wore.

"I need to go home and shower," he said calmly, as if she had just made a comment about the weather rather than demand he leave. "I'll round at the hospital, and then will be back in a little over an hour with breakfast and coffee with all the fixings. Hopefully, you'll have a better disposition at that time. Be ready to go."

Hello. Was he daft? Or just deaf? "I don't want breakfast or a better disposition." Which sounded very childish, even to her own ears. But she had a lot to deal with today and that kiss wasn't going to be added to the list. "I don't want you to come back. I want you to leave my house and never come back."

"Your car is at the funeral home. You need to eat." Could he sound any more calm? Any more logical?

"You have a long day ahead of you," he reminded her, not that she needed reminding of what the day held. "I will be back, will feed you and will drive you to the funeral home. I want to help you, Cara."

"No, you've helped enough." Lord, she didn't mean to sound so ungrateful. "Don't come back. I can feed myself." Not that she felt as if she'd ever be able to eat again with the nausea gripping her stomach. "I'll find another ride to the funeral home."

She'd walk if it meant not riding with him, not having to look at him and feel the total mortification that she felt because she'd asked him, no, begged him to stay with her because she'd been afraid to be alone. Her only excuse was that she'd been exhausted and full of grief. This morning, well, she'd thought she was kissing John. Surely. Otherwise she never would have… Oh! Why was she trying to justify her actions in her head where Sloan Trenton was concerned? She didn't owe him anything.

"Just go." She slumped forward, burying her face against her hugged-up knees.

"This is crazy, Cara," he told her gently, obviously a man of great patience. He touched her shoulder, but she couldn't bear his touch and jerked away.

"Today is going to be rough enough on both of us without you treating me like I'm your enemy," he pointed out.

He probably thought her crazy. No wonder. She thought he was a little crazy, too, for remaining so calm when she felt so…so…agitated…and aware that he was in her bed beside her. Hadn't that kiss frazzled him in the slightest?

"What is your problem with me, anyway?" He genuinely sounded confused.

"Who said I had a problem with you?" she countered, hugging her knees even tighter.

"Just a wild guess."

"Then why are you still here?" For that matter, why was she still in bed with him? Was she really so stubborn that she refused to be the one to get out of the bed when she thought he was the one who should leave?

"You asked me to stay."

Again, his calm and logic irritated her further. She glanced over at him. His expression said there was more to it and she didn't like the knowing spark in his eyes, as if he knew something she didn't.

"That was last night," she responded in as matter-of-fact way as she could manage, scooting a bit farther away from him in the bed.

"And this is this morning?"

"Exactly."

"I'll ask again, why don't you like me, Cara?"

"I don't have to have a reason, do I?"

He studied her so intently she found herself wanting to brush her fingers through her sleep-tangled hair and pinch her cheeks to give her face some color. "Most people have a reason when they dislike someone."

"You took advantage of my vulnerability last night."

"No, I didn't, and we both know it. You asked me to stay and I stayed because it seemed like the decent thing to do. You were upset."

"Staying makes me a charity case?"

"You aren't a charity case. Far, far from it." His patience seemed to wear momentarily thin. "Why are you trying to fight with me? I don't want to fight with you."

He was right. She *was* trying to fight with him.

Because she didn't like him. Because she was embarrassed by the weakness she'd shown. Because he was logical and she was totally illogical, which irritated her because really she was a logical person most of the time. Maybe.

Fighting with him was easier than addressing kissing him.

"Then leave so you won't have to fight."

He shook his head, raked his fingers through his hair. "I'd like to be beside you today."

She rose up and frowned at him. "Can you not take a hint? I don't want you beside me. Not now. Not ever. Just go."

He opened his mouth, no doubt to point out that she'd wanted him beside her the night before. She had. She couldn't deny it. The house that had been home for so many years had felt empty and creepy in the darkness when she'd known her father wasn't there.

This time she interrupted him. "I have to bury my father today. I was emotionally weak last night and asked you to stay. I shouldn't have. I admit I made a mistake. I have a boyfriend and am ashamed of my mistake, of what happened just a few minutes ago. Now I want you gone and am asking you to leave. Can you not just leave, please?"

No longer meeting her gaze, he shrugged his broad shoulders and got up from the bed on the opposite side of her. "You've made your point. I'm no longer needed or wanted." He headed for the door, pausing just inside the frame to turn to face her. "Call if you change your mind about needing a ride to the funeral home. For Preston's sake, I'll do whatever I can to make this day as easy as possible for you."

He left.

Cara burst into tears and sobbed until there were no more tears left.

When she finally got herself together enough to think about heading to the funeral home, her neighbor Gladys Jones stopped by with some homemade brownies that Cara had loved as a girl and a sympathy card. Cara requested a ride and Gladys was happy to oblige so she could question Cara on why Dr. Trenton's car had been parked in her driveway all night.

"I was too upset to drive myself home from the funeral parlor. Dr. Trenton kindly brought me home" was all she told the woman, and changed the subject time and again when Gladys kept bringing up the subject of Sloan.

The drive to the funeral home seemed to take hours rather than mere minutes. Giving Gladys a grateful hug, because really, other than the Sloan questions, she truly appreciated the woman coming to her rescue, she made her way into the funeral home, knowing the roughest day of her life awaited.

Chin high, shoulders straight, she walked into the funeral home. She could do this. She had no choice.

Everything blurred.

People greeted her, hugged her, handed her tissues when she cried. She'd not meant to cry, had kept herself together the night before at visitation, but today she cried.

Brother Elrod from her grandfather's church presented a moving message, as did the hospital's current CEO. Several suited men served as pallbearers, Sloan included, lifting the casket and assisting as it was placed inside a hearse. Then Mr. Greenwood escorted Cara to a limousine and helped her inside the impersonal black car.

The graveside service passed in just as big a blur. The local sheriff's office honored Preston's many years of serving as coroner and medical examiner and they presented Cara with a folded flag.

The late-winter wind whipped at her clothes but she felt nothing, saw nothing. Standing from her seat with legs that threatened to wobble, she dropped a single rose and a handful of dirt onto the lowered casket.

"I'm going to miss you," she whispered barely above her breath. She sucked up her grief and greeted those who remained at the graveside.

All except one person.

She just wasn't strong enough to deal with him. Or with the odd emotions that sparked in her chest every time she glanced his way.

She'd caught him watching her a few times. She hadn't been able to register if he stared at her with disgust or confusion. Probably both. No wonder. He had every right to dislike her as much as she disliked him.

Fine. She had been emotionally distraught to the point she hadn't made any rational sense that morning. She knew that. What did it matter? After this was over she never had to see the man again.

"Cara?"

But obviously he didn't intend to let today pass without one more attempt at conversation. Why? They had nothing to say to each other. The only thing they'd had in common was a man who was now being covered with reddish-brown dirt.

She didn't look at him, maybe she couldn't.

"For whatever its worth, I'm very sorry about your loss."

At Sloan's words, she glanced up, met his gaze, and got locked into those molten copper eyes. So much emo-

tion burned there. Confusion, compassion, and something so intent her knees really did wobble.

He reached out to steady her but she straightened
before he could, not wanting him to touch her.

"Thank you, Dr. Trenton. My father was a good man."
She'd given him a similar response to what she'd said
over and over to guests today.

She half expected him to say something more but
instead, his gaze still locked with hers, he just nodded. Then, breaking eye contact, he turned and walked
away from her.

Knowing it was the last time she'd ever see him, not
sure why that even mattered, she watched him walk
away, watched the strong lines of his black suit stretch
across his shoulders, watched the whip of the wind
tug at his hair. He climbed into his Jeep and she even
watched him drive away from the cemetery.

Her throat tightened and she fought back a sob. Determined not to break down in front of the few remaining people, she walked over to Mr. Greenwood.

"Can the car take me back to the funeral home now,
please?"

Once back at the funeral parlor, Mr. Greenwood informed her of incidentals, had her sign more papers,
then agreed to have all the fresh flowers delivered to
the nursing home, to have the goods boxed up and delivered to a shelter for battered women, and that he'd
have remaining food delivered to a needy family. He'd
forward all the cards to her with a description of whatever they'd been attached to written on the back so she
could send thank-you notes.

Cara went through the motions on autopilot, taking

care of what needed to be taken care of. On the outside, she figured she looked mostly together.

Good thing no one could see what her insides looked like.

She drove herself to Preston's, confirmed her flight back to New York the following morning and then paced through the big, empty house, soaking up the memories contained within its walls and yet broken-hearted that no new memories would ever be made here, no new photos would ever line the walls.

By the time she'd left for college this house had felt more a prison than a home. With each step she took, each tearful breath she sucked into her body, those same claustrophobic sensations grew.

She walked into her bedroom, glanced at the un-made bed that she'd slept in with Sloan. Would her bed smell of his spicy scent? Would she be able to sleep if she crawled between those covers alone, knowing what it had felt like to be held in his arms? To have awak-ened to his kisses?

Forget waiting until morning to fly back to New York.

She wanted out of Gloomberg. Stat.

She picked up her smartphone, pulled up her air-line's website, and, not caring at the exorbitant fees, she changed her flight to one just a few hours from the current time. No way did she want to spend the night there alone with the memories of her father or with the memories of the man she'd shared her bed with the night before.

She'd have to return soon enough to settle Preston's estate and get the few personal items she wanted to keep, but she didn't have to stay tonight. It broke her heart to think of selling the big old house, to sell his medical practice, but she wouldn't be moving back to Bloomberg. There was no need to keep any connection to the town.

She'd stay in New York, marry John and live a life far, far away from Sloan.

Um, she meant, far, far away from Gloomberg.

Then again, same difference.

She didn't like, either.

CHAPTER FOUR

THREE WEEKS LATER, Cara's Pensacola flight had been delayed over an hour. She'd had to rush the drive to Bloomberg to keep from being late to her appointment at the lawyer's office.

Although she'd known she'd have to return to Bloomberg to settle her father's estate, she'd dreaded the trip with all her being. For, oh, so many reasons that included one sexy doctor to whom she owed an apology for her overreaction to waking up beside him. All she could surmise was that she'd been exhausted and an emotional wreck. Kissing him hadn't helped matters one bit. She planned to meet with Mr. Byrd then write a short note of apology and thanks to Sloan.

But when she walked into the lawyer's office lobby and the first person she saw was Sloan sitting in the only occupied chair and reading something on his phone, all her good intentions flew out the window. She balked. "What are you doing here?"

She'd planned to make the trip without seeing him. Sure, he was the most likely candidate to buy her father's medical practice, and perhaps even his hospital shares. She'd planned to let their lawyers handle all those details. She had not wanted to actually set eyes on him.

Looking way too calm and handsome in his khakis and polo shirt, he ignored her outburst. "Good to see you again, too, Cara."

But he didn't sound as if he meant it any more than if she'd said the words to him. That was different, because before he'd been over-the-top nice. Today he seemed that if all eternity passed before he had to set eyes on her again, it would have been too soon.

"Nice to experience your sunny disposition yet again," he continued, clicking off his phone and sliding it into his khakis' front pocket.

Yep, that was definitely sarcasm.

"Mr. Byrd sent me a certified letter requesting I be here." He shrugged, as if his comment was no big deal. "So here I am."

"For the reading of my father's will?" She eyed him suspiciously. "Why would you need to be here for that?"

Looking as if she bored him, he shrugged. "Your guess is as good as mine."

She really didn't like him and his casual nonchalance. Or the fact that she'd thought of him way too often over the past few weeks. Blasted man! Yes, she'd intended to apologize for her dramatic morning show, but perhaps her antagonism toward him hadn't been so unfounded. "I doubt that."

"Same sweet Cara, I see."

"Same jerk Sloan, I see."

His brows furrowed at her comeback. He went to question her further, but Mr. Byrd stepped out from behind a door and summoned them to his office.

"I'm glad you could both be here today for the reading of Preston's will." He settled his pudgy body back into an oversize leather chair behind an equally oversize desk. "As you may know, Preston owned the house on

Maple Street, his medical practice, a significant number of hospital shares and had various investments he'd
made over the years." The man pinned them both under
his astute stare. "He died a very wealthy man."

Cara hadn't really thought of her father as wealthy,
not when he'd worked 24/7. She was glad to know that
he hadn't had to worry about money, that had he chosen to live another life he'd had that option. He'd lived
how he'd wanted, taking care of others.

Mr. Byrd scratched his balding head, looked at them
both from above the rim of his wire-framed glasses.
"Oddly enough, as fate would have it, or maybe some
sixth sense was at play, Preston changed his will about
a month ago."

A month ago? Cara's eardrums thudded with a jungle beat that warned danger lurked ahead. That would
have been at about the time of his trip to New York.
And would explain Sloan Trenton's presence in the lawyer's office.

"He came to me with some very specific changes
he wanted made to his last will and testament." He
scratched his head and avoided looking directly at Cara
as he continued. "The terms he set forth are a bit un-
usual but ironclad as I drew them up."

A sense of foreboding washed over Cara. She didn't
care about the money, would give everything away plus
everything she'd ever have to have her father back. But
to know he'd so recently changed his will, that the man
next to her had also been summoned to the lawyer's
office… Sloan had been like a son to him…

What had her father done?

And why? Had she really been that much of a disappointment to him? Or had Sloan just been that much
more the child he'd longed for?

* * *

The woman sitting in the chair next to him annoyed Sloan. Greatly. Immensely. Horrifically. She'd whipped into town, attended her father's funeral, blown out quicker than expected and left a tornado's worth of aftermath in Sloan's life.

Because he hadn't been able to stop thinking about her.

Which was crazy. She wasn't a nice woman, had been outright rude to him, used him, then cast him aside, unaware of how much havoc she'd caused. Preston's daughter or not, he should dislike her.

He did dislike her.

Greatly. Immensely. Horrifically. That's what the strong emotions that being near her again evoked within him. *Dislike.*

"Those terms are?" Cara asked, sounding more like a businesswoman than a doctor.

"That Mr. Sloan Trenton is to inherit one half of Preston's medical practice and one half of all real property attached to that business."

Cara's throat worked, but she didn't speak. She didn't have to. Sloan knew what she was thinking, saw out of the corner of his eye how her fingers bit into the edge of her chair.

Mr. Byrd looked directly at Sloan. "He'd planned to eventually sell half the practice to you and make you a partner in the fullest sense. He wanted to ensure that still happened, even if something happened to him, so he'd know Bloomberg would be looked after in his absence."

Sloan was floored. And humbled. He'd figured he'd buy Preston's practice from Little Miss Sunshine or that she'd refuse to sell to him and he'd just open his own practice in Bloomberg. Never had he considered that Preston would give him half of what he'd spent a lifetime building. Never would Sloan have agreed to his doing so. That the man he'd loved had wanted him to have half the practice filled him with so many emotions, including awkwardness, that Preston would have done such a generous thing.

How his heart ached that Preston was gone, that he wasn't there for him to tell him how much his actions meant, not the actual gifts but that Preston would do that for him, a poor kid from nowhere street, Cincinnati, who'd never had anyone really care for him… Sloan took a deep breath, thinking how blessed he'd been to have been a part of such a great man's life, to have loved and have been loved by such greatness, and wished he'd had more time to soak in everything he could learn from Preston.

Cara's gasp, then the clamping tight of her lips told him she was a bit floored by Preston's will change as well. But not in quite the same way as Sloan. No doubt she'd see Preston's actions as the ultimate betrayal or something that Sloan himself had fostered into happening. He hadn't. Not ever had he even dreamed of such a thing. Dreamed? Losing his mentor and dearest friend was a nightmare.

Cara quickly composed herself. Hands folded in her lap, she gave a tight smile to the lawyer. "With the way my father loved this town and respected Dr. Trenton, I can certainly understand that he'd want to ensure he stayed in Bloomberg to carry on his practice."

"Very true," the lawyer agreed, as if his revelation hadn't caused such a torrent of mixed emotions to burst free in the room. "Those were almost Preston's exact words when he came to me to change his will."

Still reeling at the enormity of Preston's gift from the grave, Sloan's ears roared. He wouldn't have left Bloomberg. Preston had known that Sloan had found a peace in the town that he'd never known elsewhere. For the first time in his life, Sloan had belonged and felt a part of something larger than himself, a medical family, a community, a town. He belonged here and would die here. Preston had known that.

"And the remainder of my father's assets?" Cara's voice was as smooth as silk, no inflection of emotion one way or the other. Those fingers in her lap worked overtime, though, clenching into her palm and straightening over and over. Whether she was making an angry fist or releasing nervous energy, Sloan couldn't say for sure.

Mr. Byrd leaned back in his leather chair and met Cara's gaze head on with a steely light that Sloan had never seen the man have before. The look was probably his courtroom, questioning-an-opposing-witness look. Certainly, many a lesser person than Cara Conner would have squirmed under that gaze. She didn't. Other than the fingers, she was the picture of calm, cool and collected.

Was she even aware she was making the telltale finger motions?

"You inherit the other half of Preston's practice and all his other possessions so long as you meet certain conditions." The lawyer paused dramatically, the conditions weighing heavily in the air.

Despite the roaring still taking place within his own skull, Sloan could almost hear the wheels turning in Cara's head.

"What conditions?" Annoyance laced her question.

"Like I said, Preston was very specific about the

terms of his will." The lawyer straightened a stack of papers on his desk that hadn't needed straightening, then he fixed that courtroom look on Cara again. "You have to move to Bloomberg, live in Preston's house and work at the clinic with Sloan for a minimum of forty hours a week for a minimum of six months."

"I can't move here," she gasped, her face contorted with horror and all pretense of composure gone. She gripped the edge of the desk and leaned toward the lawyer. "I don't want to live here. I won't live here. I hate this place."

She shook her head, as if trying to clear what the lawyer had said.

"Hate away." Mr. Byrd didn't seem to care one way or the other. "But not living in Bloomberg is not an option if you want to meet the terms of your father's will. You have to reside in the Maple Street residence for six months."

"I don't want any of his possessions, anyway. I'd planned to sell everything," she said, probably thinking out loud more than actually telling them her intentions.

The lawyer shook his head. "Nothing is yours to sell until the will's conditions are met. After they've been met, you can sell or do whatever you want to with his assets."

Sloan felt Cara's animosity bristling next to him, had a horrible inkling as to what more the lawyer was going to say. *Oh, Preston, what have you done?*

"If I refuse to meet the conditions of his will? Then what? Where do my father's assets go? To charity or perhaps another one of his causes?" Each word sounded ripped from between her tight lips.

"Your father set up trusts for his charities many years ago," Mr. Byrd informed her smoothly. "He formed those trusts as separate entities and they are well taken care of."

Sloan knew Preston had sponsored several local scholarships, kids' clubs and who knew what all other things. Preston's involvement in the community and his determination to make a difference with the Bloomberg community had been just one of the many things he'd admired about the man.

"If you fail to meet the terms of your father's will, Dr. Trenton inherits the clinic, the clinic's real property and your father's other assets, including the house on Maple Street and his vast investments."

Cara's jaws ground together with a loud snap, but she only said, "What? He has no conditions to meet? No jumping into burning buildings to save small children or stopping out-of-control speeding locomotives?"

The lawyer's eyes darkened with displeasure at her sarcasm, but he maintained his professionalism. "Dr. Trenton has no conditions to meet, other than that Preston hoped he'd continue to live in Bloomberg and provide medical care for the community. He trusted that he would."

Cara stood from her seat, moved across the room, then faced the lawyer. Her body shook beneath the cool lines of her skirt and blouse. Not that Sloan was looking that closely at her body. At least, he was trying not to. Hard not to at least be aware of where she paced when she aimed so much animosity at him that at any moment she might launch herself at him in anger.

"Those terms are ridiculous," she said. "I can't imagine them holding up in a real court of law. I live in New York. I have a life there. My father knew that." Her gaze settled onto Sloan and pure hatred shone in her blue-green eyes.

Not looking concerned or surprised by her out-burst, Mr. Byrd shrugged. "I can give you several at-torneys' names if you'd like to pursue contesting the will. However, I should advise you that Dr. Conner left no loopholes. The terms will hold up in court and will be carried out as he wished. I gave my friend my word on that and will personally do all I can, including calling in favors at any level necessary, to ensure my friend's last wishes are adhered to." The man gave her a dis-approving look. "I'd have thought you'd want to honor your father's dying request, but perhaps his wishes for your future don't matter so much when you have your own life to live."

Cara winced at the man's wounding words. Sloan suspected they carried a whopping, salty sting to her raw emotions. Sloan didn't doubt that Cara had loved her father. He'd seen and heard Preston talk about her too much to think that. They'd been close in their own way. No doubt, Preston having changed his will had shocked her, irritated her as it was her father manipu-lating her from the grave to do what he'd been unable to convince her to do while he'd been alive.

Sloan understood her frustration. He wouldn't have wanted to be manipulated, either, from the grave or otherwise. He'd never wanted or expected anything to be handed to him. He'd paid his way in life and had no problem with continuing to do so. He'd tell her that, but her gaze had narrowed with something akin to pure hatred as she stared at him.

"You knew this? That my father had changed his will?"

"Preston and I never talked money unless it had to do with the clinic." True. He and Preston had got along fabulously and had never had cross words. He directed his attention to the lawyer sitting across the desk. "Can I refuse the terms of the will? As long as she is willing to sell me the clinic and Preston's hospital shares at a fair market price, Cara can have everything. The clinic and hospital shares are all I'm interested in and I'll gladly pay for those."

"You can refuse the terms of the will, but Preston's estate would sit untouched for the full six months and an additional six months. After a year had passed, all his belongings would then be auctioned off to the highest bidder. The terms he set forth in his will not being honored would be a disgrace, considering everything Preston was in this community. This is what he wanted. His wishes should be honored." The lawyer's gaze cut to Cara in blatant disapproval of her wanting to fight her father's terms. "By both of you. If for no other reason than out of love and respect for a great man who has made his final wishes known."

Still visibly agitated, Cara sank back into the chair next to Sloan's and gave the lawyer a confused look. "Judge me all you want, but I can't just move to lower Alabama. Real life doesn't work that way. I have a job, responsibilities in New York."

"Why not?"

At his question, she spun towards Sloan. "You stay out of this. You...you...home wrecker."

Taken aback, Sloan flinched at her venom. "Huh?"

Mr. Byrd watched them curiously. Sloan was pretty curious himself. Why would anyone ever call him a home wrecker, particularly Cara? She'd not ever lived in Bloomberg during the same time he had. It would be near impossible to wreck a home that she'd already left for greener pastures years before.

Although perhaps that was unfair. Cara had left

Bloomberg for medical school then had stayed to do a job she loved in a place she'd also professed to love. As an adult she'd had that right. Just because Preston had wanted her home, in Bloomberg, didn't mean Cara had been wrong to live her own life and make her own decisions about where she wanted to live.

Sloan even understood her frustration with Preston's will. From the grave, Preston, thinking he knew best, was manipulating his daughter to do what he'd wanted all along. Cara to return home and work at his clinic.

How many times had he heard Preston say his girl was too stubborn for her own good? That she needed to come home and take her rightful place at the clinic?

One way or the other, Preston had been determined to prove his point to Cara by forcing her to be in Bloomberg.

Which meant she'd be working with him.

As if Cara didn't already detest him, Preston had made him the enemy.

Which meant six months of his life would be in constant turmoil.

He didn't want Preston's money. He also didn't want Cara at the clinic. Their last encounter had left a bad taste in his mouth. One he'd not really recovered from yet.

"Fine." Cara's voice had taken on a detached quality. "He can have my father's worldly possessions. They are just things. I'll move my personal items out of the house and Dr. Trenton can do whatever he wishes with the rest."

"I'm sorry, Miss Conner," Mr. Byrd apologized without really looking sorry at all. Actually, there was a steely spark to his gaze that said he enjoyed putting the squeeze on another human being and especially on Cara as she wasn't giving in to her father's maneuvering. "But if you decline the terms of the will, you are giving up your rights to any of Preston's possessions, including all personal items within the Maple Street home."

"What?" Cara's jaw dropped. Her face pale, she shook her head in denial. "This isn't happening."

Sloan didn't budge in his chair, just watched the events unfold between Preston's lawyer and his daughter. Tension gurgled between them to the point that had they come to physical blows he wouldn't have been surprised.

"You've not lived in that house for several years and therefore all items inside the house would be considered part of Preston's estate and not yours to take."

Cara's bravado sailed out of her on a puff of wind that expressed itself as a pained sigh. "I can't get my things? My mother's things? Her photos and diaries?"

The lawyer leaned forward, stared directly into her eyes, and sealed their fate. "If you decline the will's terms, those items would be Dr. Trenton's things, not yours. Anything you removed from the house would be theft and punishable by law as such."

"Theft?" She blinked, her hands visibly shaking in her lap. Sloan doubted there had been many times in Cara's life when someone had caught her so off guard, but, to give her credit, she had dealt with a lot over the past few weeks.

"Oh, yes. If you take a single item out of that house, it is my duty to have you arrested for theft of property from the estate of Dr. Preston Conner."

"You have got to be kidding me." She blinked as if she were caught up in some crazy movie plot. Sloan understood. He felt that way, too. Actually, he felt sorry for Cara, even though he knew he shouldn't. What had Preston done?

"I assure you, this is no joke."

"Can I purchase the items I want from the estate?"

"Perhaps Dr. Trenton would consider selling you any item of particular interest that you would like. But Preston was a wise man and did leave specifics on that, as well. A year would have to pass prior to Dr. Trenton being able to sell any item from the estate and any sale would have to be via a public auction or bid."

Any moment Sloan expected the top of Cara's head to explode. Literally. He wouldn't blame her. Preston had thought of everything.

Her face had gone from pale to puffy and quite pink. Her hands still fisted and unfisted. Sloan wasn't sure if she wanted to deck the lawyer, him or perhaps her late father.

"Is that everything?" Cara asked, shuffling some papers Mr. Byrd handed her and readying herself to leave the lawyer's office.

"Not quite." Oh, yeah, the lawyer was enjoying this way too much, Sloan thought as he smiled ever so slyly and pulled out two manila envelopes. "Preston left notes to you both."

Cara's head shot up and her breath caught. "He left notes?"

"Yes."

She closed her eyes, took a deep breath. "Were they from before he made the changes or at the time?"

"He gave me both notes in sealed envelopes on the day he signed and put into effect his new will."

Sloan eyed the lawyer, wondering at what further craziness was going to unfold. "You don't know what they say?"

"I've an idea, but no, I haven't read the specific messages. The letters are for the eyes of the beholder only, not mine or anyone else's. That's what Preston wanted and I respect him enough to honor his wishes." The man's inferences couldn't be missed. He handed Cara a sealed envelope with her name written in Preston's bold handwriting on the front.

Sloan watched her gaze go to her name, watched her visually trace Preston's handwriting and then her fingertip followed suit. Her hands shook slightly and he could only imagine the emotions flooding through her. His own hands probably shook, too. He took his letter and tried not to let his own sentimentality get to him. No way would he let Cara know how much all this affected him.

Inside the envelope was his final message from the man he'd loved more than any other person his entire life. Why did he suspect he already knew what his message would be? That somehow his message would echo Preston's final verbal plea to him? That Cara would be involved and that if he wasn't careful she would destroy the life he had made for himself in Bloomberg?

Just look at how one night in the woman's arms had torn him to bits a few weeks ago. Still tore him up. If he'd had any doubt, seeing her walk into the lawyer's office had set him straight. She messed with his head big time.

Even now the cherry candy scent of her filled his nostrils and made him want to lean closer and inhale as much of her as his lungs would hold. Quite literally, she drove him crazy.

A man could only stand so much.

Without another word, he got up, envelope in hand,

and walked out of the lawyer's office. Let them devise whatever they wanted.

He wasn't playing their game.

Cara had instantly disliked Sloan. She just hadn't fully understood how deep that dislike was destined to run.

She didn't need her father's money. With her scholarships, she'd graduated debt-free and had a great job in the emergency room. She had a good life.

Had had a good life.

Because when she'd gone back to New York after her father's funeral, she hadn't been the same.

Had found herself more and more annoyed with John and his lack of attention to their relationship. He talked big, but no action. No ring on her finger. Problem was, she wasn't even sure she wanted a ring. She'd thought she had, but when she closed her eyes, it wasn't John's kisses that haunted her dreams. The kisses of a man she couldn't stand had stolen her breath and her sleeping fantasies. The way he'd held her, the way his body had moved against hers, the intensity with which he'd kissed her…

Ugh. She just wanted to forget him. Everything about him.

But, according to Mr. Byrd, she could choose to either work with Sloan for six months or say goodbye to everything from her childhood—her mother's paintings, her mother's wedding dress, her mother's diaries, her mother's china, her mother's hope chest, which had been Cara's grandmother's. All material things, but things with such great sentimental value that Cara felt a bit bereft just at the thought of not having them to pass on to her own children someday so they'd have a physical piece of their grandmother to hold on to and know the vivacious woman she'd been prior to Gloomberg sucking the life out of her. Her mother must be rolling over in her grave that Cara's father was forcing her to return to the town.

Her father had wanted her to just up and leave her life and play at living her daddy's dream for her.

She glanced at the lawyer, who still watched her closely. "I had planned on staying for a couple of days to sort through the items I wanted to take back to New York with me. Is it okay for me to stay in the house or do I need to move into a hotel?"

"No hotel is necessary, but you can't remove any of the items from the house. Not for a year."

"Yes, I think you've made that point clear already." She sounded snappy and knew it, but the man had just destroyed her life. "The terms of my father's will really aren't fair, Mr. Byrd."

"It's not my job to judge my client's final wishes, just to carry them out. He wanted you in Bloomberg and used every means at his disposal to make that happen. Perhaps, before you make any decisions, you need to think long and hard about that."

Her father had made his wishes known, had left no doubt how he wanted her to spend her life, that he felt her own choices were wrong.

"You're right. I do need to think about all the things you've said."

It would be so easy to just say okay, to give in to the terms he'd set forth and live in Bloomberg for six months.

Yet it wouldn't be easy at all.

She'd give up everything if she accepted the terms— the job she loved, her relationship with John, because no way would he agree to her moving to Bloomberg for six months, her Manhattan apartment, which was so fabulously located and quite a find. When her six months were up, she'd have to start over completely with her career and her personal life.

But could she really say no to her father's final request of her?

How could she say yes?

She stood, nodded at the lawyer. "I'll stay at my father's tonight as planned and will be in touch within the next couple of days to let you know my decision."

"You have thirty days to decide."

She shook her head. "I won't need thirty days, because I can't throw away my life to move back to Bloomberg."

But could she really throw away her past?

"Bloomberg isn't so bad."

"That is a matter of opinion." She gave him a tight smile.

"Your father was a brilliant man and he chose Bloomberg. He loved this town and there were reasons for that. Reasons you may not know or understand because you never attempted to. Perhaps, while deciding your future, you should stop and ask yourself why not."

My dearest Cara,

If you are reading this, then I've gone on to a better place. I don't want you to mourn me or to be sad, because I've lived a good life. I've loved in ways most men never love—your mother and you.

Isabelle never adjusted to small-town life as I'd hoped she would, but you already know that. You have fashioned your life around wanting to be like her. It took me a long time to realize that, to understand that.

As you decide your future course, I'm asking—
no, begging—you to fashion your life around
wanting to be like me, even if for only six months.
Six months is not a long time in the grand scheme
of life. Yet six months can change the way a person sees the world, the way a young woman sees
herself and her place in the world.

I know you, Cara. I know you're contemplat-
ing walking away from Bloomberg. Give me
six months to show you my world, to show you
Bloomberg through my eyes. Afterwards, if you
still want to leave, then go, have no regrets and
know you have my blessing in doing so.

I love you, my daughter. I have from the moment you entered the world and I always will.

Dad

Tears streamed down Cara's cheeks. Her eyes stung.
Her cheeks hurt. She drowned on postnasal drainage
from sobbed-back tears.

No. He couldn't do this to her. He just couldn't.

She didn't want to live in Bloomberg.

How could she not?

Not so she could inherit his assets, but because if she
didn't his words, his last request of her, would haunt
her all the days of her life.

Whether she wanted to move to Bloomberg and step
into her father's world or not, for six months she was
going to.

She'd lived in Bloomberg eighteen years. Being back
six months wasn't going to change the way she looked
at this town or at herself.

She'd carry out her father's request, but at the end of
six months she'd leave and never look back.

CHAPTER FIVE

"WE GAVE YOU two slots per patient all week to give extra time to learn the patients, the electronic medical record and the way the office runs. I wish you'd been able to arrive earlier so you could have had the opportunity to meet everyone and get your feet wet prior to starting today," Amie Matthews informed Cara four weeks later on a bright and early Monday morning as they walked toward the back of the clinic. "Other than the EMR, it's not that different from when you hung out here as a girl, but there are some changes. Like doing everything on the computer rather than with paper."

There had been a lot of reasons why Cara hadn't arrived earlier. Mainly, she hadn't wanted to get her feet wet until the clock started ticking on her six months. Today was that day. *Tick. Tick. Tick.* Time flew when one was having fun. Did that mean the next six months was going to drag by?

"Your schedule is full but shouldn't be too bad today," Amie assured her, smiling in a familiar way that used to set Cara at ease. Now she suspected everyone at the clinic just wanted her to finish her time, sell Sloan the clinic and her be done with Bloomberg.

"They started booking the moment we added your name to the schedule, you know." Amie reached out, touched Cara's arm with gentle reassurance. "I think almost everyone just wants to come in and tell you how much they miss your father."

"Possibly." She smiled at the woman who had been her father's nurse for a good twenty years. Amie Matthews had probably known Preston Conner better than anyone other than Cara…and maybe Sloan.

Sloan. She'd not seen him since he'd walked out of the lawyer's office. She'd not even talked to him. Mr. Byrd had handled letting Sloan know that she'd decided she could take a six-month hiatus from her real life to fulfill her father's last request.

In the grand scheme of life, what was six months when it gave her the peace of mind and heart that she'd abided by her father's last wish?

She'd spoken with Amie and with Erica, the office manager, several times over the past couple of weeks as they'd made arrangements for her to join the practice and be official with various state health boards and insurance companies.

"What are you planning to do about the hospital?"

She was sure she'd forgotten a dozen things in her whirlwind relocation, but the hospital wasn't one of them. "The board met last week and approved my privileges. Mr. Byrd and Erica handled all the paperwork on this end. She's great, by the way."

"She has done a great job managing the practice," Amie agreed. "Your father can really pick good help." Amie drew in a deep breath that was full of sorrow then pasted her smile back onto her face. "Thank goodness you have your privileges. Dr. Trenton is spread too thin between here and the hospital. Casey, our nurse practitioner, is great, but she hasn't been able to lighten his load nearly enough."

"I met her when I was home last year." That would have been right before Sloan had started at the practice. Her father had hired his wonder boy but Sloan hadn't arrived in Bloomberg yet.

"She's a gem. As is Sloan."

Of course Sloan was a gem. Everyone thought so.

Her astute eyes studying her too closely, Amie smiled at Cara with the same friendliness and motherly affection she'd always shown her. "You'll like working with him, Cara. We all do. He's a good doctor. He's a lot like your father."

Cara closed her eyes. She was tired of hearing how much Sloan was like her father. She was tired of hearing about him, period. All morning she'd dreaded seeing him.

And yet... That achy, nervous feeling in the pit of her stomach was dread, right? Not excitement. Not anticipation. Not curiosity that perhaps she had overbuilt the man's looks, aura and kissing ability in her mind. Not curiosity and anxiety over how he'd walked out of Mr. Byrd's office. None of those things. Just dread.

She glanced down the office hallway, wondering where the dreaded doctor was, why she hadn't yet seen him. She wanted to get that first meeting over with, to know how he was going to react to her being at the office, invading his space, for the next six months.

Sure, from the moment she'd let Mr. Byrd know that she was going to fulfill the terms of her father's will, no doubt Sloan had known she'd be in Bloomberg, would be working at the clinic. Had he been disappointed at her decision? Of course he had. He had everything to gain by her staying right where she'd been.

Her decision wasn't based on money. She just hadn't been able to stomach the thought of disappointing her father that one last time, of possibly losing her mother's things, of losing her few prized family heirlooms.

Too bad if Sloan Trenton didn't like her decision.

Amie followed her gaze and her smile grew a little too pleased for Cara's comfort. "He texted a little while ago to say he'd gotten hung up at the hospital but that he'd be here as quickly as he could. He's killing himself, trying to keep everything going. I'm so glad you're here. Only I wish…" Amie stopped, her smile completely gone. She winced a little. Cara didn't need her to finish to know what her father's nurse had been going to say. Only she wished it had been sooner, had been while Preston had still been alive, that her father was there to show Cara the ropes, so to speak, as she stepped into her new career.

A smidge of guilt hit Cara. She hadn't thought about Sloan carrying two doctors' loads by himself.

She had thought about Sloan, though.

Way too often she'd thought about the dark-haired man with his mesmerizing copper eyes. She'd thought about waking in his arms and the passion of his kisses. She'd thought about the fact that for six months she'd be thrown together with him. She'd thought about the look of disgust on his face when he'd walked out of Mr. Byrd's office and how that look had punched her in the gut. How had he dared to look upset when she was the one who was drastically changing her life?

But not once had she thought about how her father's death had affected him and his workload. She'd been too caught up in her own grief and life changes and how she felt emotionally blackmailed into returning to a town that had robbed her of her family. Was she really that selfish? Since when had she quit caring about others? Quit recognizing their needs?

Still, she couldn't have gotten relocated much quicker. She'd had to work out her notice in the emergency room, had had to pack her New York life, take care of the legalities of practicing medicine in another state and so forth. She'd come as quickly as she could. Mostly so she could get these six months behind her and then figure out what was next for her.

She'd broken things off with John—why hadn't he cared more at the demise of their relationship? For that matter, why hadn't she? She'd been with the man for years, yet walking away hadn't hurt. She'd thought she was going to spend the rest of her life with him. Walking away should have at least stung a little. It hadn't. He'd even helped her pack and driven her to the airport. They'd parted as friends. If there had been passion, shouldn't he have been begging her to stay? Shouldn't she have been running back from her airport gate and flinging herself into his arms for one last kiss?

Leaving him had been all too easy. For both of them.

She took a deep breath. No time to think about John right now. Today she started her six-month penitence. She'd suck up her grief over her lost life and she'd make the best of the next six months, whether Sloan liked it or not.

"He loved your father, you know."

Amie's words cut into Cara's thoughts. Bitterness burned the back of her throat. "So I've been told."

"He did. Just as Preston loved him like the son he never had."

At any moment a hole was going to appear in her throat from the acid gnawing away at her. She ignored the sharp pain that ate at her body, met Amie's eyes, and changed the subject before she said something she'd regret. "Are you working as my nurse today? If so, I imagine we should get started because it may take me a bit to pick up this EMR system."

In fact, Conner Medical Clinic's charting system wasn't too different from what Cara had used during one of her residencies. Although she asked Amie question after question, she muddled her way through her morning patients. All without so much as a glimpse of Sloan.

How lucky was she?

At lunch, when Cara went back into her father's office—her office—she stopped at the fresh bouquet of flowers on the desk. Had Sloan...?

"We wanted you to know how glad we are to have you at the clinic," a petite brunette said from behind her, stopping Cara's train of thought. "I'm Casey Watson, by the way. We met briefly when you were home last and again at the funeral home, but I'm not sure if you remember me."

Cara shook the woman's outstretched hand. "Sure I do. You were all aglow because you'd just gotten back from your vacation and talked to me about Aruba. John and I ended up going there for a long weekend a few months after that."

"That's right." Casey's smile brightened. "Hope you enjoyed it as much as I did. That was the best vacation I've ever had. Wish I was there now."

Actually, John had gotten a bit of food poisoning and they had spent a great deal of the weekend just lounging around the hotel. Cara had been bored, but had caught up on some reading.

"Are you talking about going on vacation again?"

Cara's breath caught and her gaze immediately went to the man who'd spoken and was leaning against the office door frame. Her imagination hadn't built up a thing. The man was beautiful in every sense of the word. "Sloan."

Saying his name out loud couldn't be appropriate but it popped out of Cara's mouth all the same.

Sloan had avoided bumping into Cara all morning. That hadn't given him as much peace as it should have, though, because he'd still known she was in the building, that for the next six months she'd be a constant thorn in his side.

Actually, it wasn't his side that she pricked but a spot deep in his chest. How could you be half-crazy about someone you'd never met in person? How could you meet that person and instantly trigger such dislike? How could you shove that person out of your thoughts when you realized that your infatuation had been silly and that you weren't even sure you actually liked the person?

Almost a month had passed since he'd seen her last and yet Sloan still hadn't figured out the answers to any of the questions that had plagued him since Preston's funeral.

Preston. Lord, how he missed that man. Would a time ever come that he'd wake up and not instantly recall that Preston had gone on to a better place? That he wouldn't relive a moment of grief and loss every single day?

"Yeah, well, it was a really great vacation. You should have been there," Casey said, smiling at Sloan as if he hung the moon. She usually did. He thought of her as his kid sister.

"I have this feeling that if I'd been there you wouldn't have had nearly as much fun as you claim to have had."

Casey's face flushed a pretty pink. She hadn't mentioned meeting anyone while she'd been in Aruba for a medical continuing education seminar, but Sloan felt

confident she had spent the week with some lucky guy.
Regardless, whatever had happened, Casey never mentioned anything other than to talk about what a great
vacation she'd had.

"You might be right," Casey agreed, standing up
from where she perched against Cara's desk. "The reality is that you have to butter me up with the promise
of upcoming vacations so I'll keep coming in to work
day after day. Otherwise I'd likely just stay at home and
avoid this craziness we call medicine."

Knowing Casey loved her career as much as he did,
Sloan put his hand over his heart and feigned devastation. "A woman who chooses vacations over me. Say
it isn't so."

He and Casey both laughed, but Cara just watched
their byplay with narrowed eyes. His gaze went beyond
her to the photos hanging on Preston's office wall. What
had happened to the smiley, adventurous woman from
all the pictures? Did she really dislike this town so much
that she would wear a constant scowl for the next six
months? Or was it just him she disliked so much? Preston's will couldn't have helped the situation.

Turning his attention back to Casey, he grinned
and was grateful at least one of his coproviders was
all smiles. "For the record, I really appreciate you putting your scheduled vacation on hold. I'd have been lost
without you last week." He winked at her but remained
aware of Cara watching them.

"Yeah, yeah," Casey agreed, laughing then taking
on a somber look. "You know I wouldn't leave you
with Preston…" She glanced at Cara. "I'm really sorry
about your father."

Cara's face instantly blanched. Nothing impassive
about her expression now.

She closed her eyes and took a deep breath.

Before Cara could reply, Casey's cell phone beeped. She excused herself, but not before adding, "So glad you are here as part of our family, Cara. As you can probably already tell, we are one big family. If you need anything, let me know. I'll help if I can."

Then left Cara and Sloan alone.

Except for the other six or seven people in the building of course. But alone in Preston's office—Cara's office.

Which suddenly felt very awkward. After avoiding her all morning, after keeping all contact they'd had through the lawyer's office, why had he come to her office to look for her?

Why did he always feel so flustered around her? Because of what Preston had asked of him?

"I'm headed over to the hospital to check on a patient I admitted last night for gastroenteritis and dehydration." He gave her what he hoped was a peace-offering smile. "Do you want to go with me?"

She blinked her wide eyes as if he'd sprouted a horn from his forehead. "Why would I want to do that?"

Why? He could give her a hundred different reasons, but he didn't utter a single one. Just waited. Whatever Preston's note to his daughter had said, it certainly hadn't tamped down her anger towards him. If anything, she looked at him with even more dislike than she had that day in Mr. Byrd's office.

"Why wouldn't you want to do that? You are going to work in this office for six months. Learning the ropes from me seems a logical decision."

"I could give you a hundred different reasons why going with you wouldn't be a logical decision at all. Plus, I'm not a newbie. I've been working in a busy emergency department for almost a year now. It's not like I'm wet behind the ears."

"You're a prickly thing, aren't you?" Sloan laughed at hearing her say his own thoughts out loud, only in reverse. He had the feeling they were going to be at opposite ends of the spectrum a lot. Which was going to make for a long six months. Preston's stubborn blood ran red through her. No doubt he'd be the one to have to offer the olive branch. For Preston's sake and for the sake of them all, he'd offer her the whole olive tree if it meant she'd relax a little.

Her forehead wrinkled. "What's so funny?"

Taking a deep breath, he shook his head and decided to put the cards on the table. "Look, Cara, whether we like our current situation or not, for the next six months we are going to be working together. Those six months will go much smoother, for us and for those who work here with us, if we can find some level of peace between us. If you want to hate me outside the office, fine. Hate away. But here at the office let's at least call a truce, because I don't think the others will understand if we're constantly at odds."

She walked away from him, went behind the desk, put her hands on the chair back, and took a deep breath. "You're right."

She didn't look happy. He suspected that having to admit he was right had a lot to do with her displeasure. Still, it was more than she'd given him up to this point.

"So," he ventured. "I'll ask again, do you want to go to the hospital with me to see a patient I admitted last night for twenty-three-hour observation and IV fluids? I can walk you through normal protocol at Bloomberg General Hospital, because I imagine Bloomberg is going to be vastly different than working in a busy emergency department in Manhattan."

Her fingers dug into the leather of her father's chair, her knuckles blanching white. "I suppose that would be the logical thing for me to do."

"It would."

She took a deep breath, nodded her head. "Okay. Let's go so you can show me the ropes."

He'd half expected her to refuse, but maybe she was going to meet him halfway so the next six months would pass without either of them being too scathed.

Maybe.

The awkward silence that ensued wasn't promising, though. She was just as lost in her thoughts as he was in his.

"What did you think of your first morning?" he asked as they walked toward the hospital, searching for something to break the tension. Preston had built his office on a piece of property adjacent to the hospital, which simplified the sometimes frequent trips back and forth to check on patients.

"I didn't kill anyone," she said drily.

"Good to know, especially since the most likely victim would have been me."

She stopped in midstep, causing Sloan to do the same. Color infused her face and her lips compressed tightly.

"Hmm, I better behave or you may not be able to say the same about your afternoon, eh? You didn't have any Mafia connections in New York, did you?"

"Just a few," she quipped, still not moving. The light breeze caught a loose strand of her caught-up red hair and whipped it across her porcelain face. "I really don't like you, you know."

He knew. "Exactly my point."

"You're not helping."

A smidge of guilt hit Sloan. "This is me trying to be helpful and break the ice between us, Cara. I don't want the next six months to be miserable for either of us."

"Seriously?" She eyed him suspiciously.

"Seriously. I know we got off to a bad start, which I don't fully understand since you didn't like me from the moment I showed up on your doorstep. But, for whatever it's worth, I am glad you are here. The past few weeks have been hellish."

As her scowl lifted and her expression softened, he admitted that he was very glad. Because, whether he understood it or not, Cara Conner got under his skin and he had six months to pry her out from under there and lose his fascination with her. Plus convince her to stay in Bloomberg forever. No big deal.

"I'm sorry you've had to carry my father's load for the past couple of months, Sloan." Her gaze met his and her eyes flashed with guilt. "I had things I had to resolve in New York before I could get here."

Her sincerity and how it hit him suggested everything about her was a big deal. A very big deal.

"I've managed, but, like I said, I am glad you're here. Truce?"

Her gaze narrowed with obvious displeasure at their situation, but then she stuck out her hand. "Truce, but I still don't like you, much less trust you. You have a lot to gain by my failing."

He laughed. "Well, at least that's a start and in case you weren't paying attention, I didn't ask for this situation to be thrust on us any more than you did. I cared enough for Preston to want his final wishes carried out, which means I don't want you to fail at all."

CHAPTER SIX

SELFISHNESS WASN'T SOMETHING Cara associated with herself, but apparently she should have. With her father and with Sloan. All she'd thought about had been how her father had forced her into six months of hell. Not once had she considered that he'd also forced Sloan into six months of limbo. Or hell, since he was forced to work with her and she was miserable about the whole thing and apparently determined to make him just as much so.

Maybe he really hadn't dropped hints to her father that he was like a son to him and should be treated as such. Preston hadn't been a foolish, gullible man. Obviously, Sloan had impressed him and won his favor.

Still, she didn't trust him. Shouldn't trust him. But for six months she would be working with him in a close-knit environment and would be fulfilling her father's final wishes. She'd quit being such a Negative Nancy about the whole thing.

He chatted while they walked into the hospital, introducing her to people left and right as if she hadn't lived here eighteen years. She just smiled and carried on, accepting more condolences for her loss.

"Miranda, this is Dr. Conner," Sloan introduced Cara

as they entered the hospital patient room. A pale young girl stared back at them.

"I thought Dr. Conner..." the girl's voice trailed off.

"He did," Sloan continued, smiling gently at the young woman. "This is his daughter, Cara. She's going to be in Bloomberg, helping out at her father's clinic for a while."

She nodded and smiled weakly at Cara.

"Nice to meet you," she told the patient, whom she actually didn't know, and joined Sloan at the computer as he pulled up lab results.

"Am I going to get to go home, Dr. Trenton?" the woman asked in a voice still so weak it should have answered her question for her.

"Not today, Miranda. Your electrolytes are still too low, despite the supplements we've infused. Your potassium has only come up a few points from two point nine to three point one. I'm going to have another bag of potassium infused in hopes of getting you up within normal range."

"Is that why I still feel so weak?"

He nodded and, after skimming over her other lab results, moved to the hospital bed. "It is. I suspect your muscles are still cramping, too."

Miranda winced. "I got an awful 'charley horse' during the night. It woke me up and I had to call the nurse to help me."

"Those should stop once we get your potassium back to normal. Now that your stomach symptoms have resolved I'm hopeful this next bag will do the trick."

"I hope so."

"Me, too." Sloan leaned forward and placed his stethoscope diaphragm on her chest. He listened to her heart, lungs,and abdomen, then palpated her abdomen. "Any pain?"

"Just that cramping sensation before I have a bowel movement, but it's better than it was."

Cara clicked on the radiology file and reviewed Miranda's computerized tomography scan of her abdomen and pelvis. "I see she had ovarian cysts that showed up."

"They were an incidental finding but, yes, there were ovarian cysts bi-lat. No gallbladder disease or appendix issues were seen."

Cara felt silly for having pointed out the positive findings to him when he'd obviously already looked over the results.

"Thanks for the heads-up," he told her, meeting her gaze and smiling.

Her breath caught. Okay, he was determined to be nice to her when really he could make the next six months so much worse, when he could make them so unbearable that she'd just leave, and then he'd inherit all her father's assets. But that wasn't what he was doing. He was being nice to her. Even when she hadn't been nice to him.

Ugh.

The man had her emotions torn every which way. He was her enemy and yet…he wasn't acting like an enemy at all.

The following morning, Sloan popped his head into Cara's office, catching her studying her computer screen. "Thanks for checking on Miranda this morning."

"You're welcome. I was hoping she'd be well enough to discharge this morning after you gave her the extra fluids and electrolytes yesterday, but she was still pretty weak. Her white blood count had jumped up to fifteen thousand this morning."

Sloan arched a brow. "What do you think is up with that?"

"I'm not sure. I've ordered a round of antibiotics and a repeat blood count to be drawn. If her numbers are still up or if her symptoms worsen, I think we should repeat imaging."

He nodded. "Sounds like a good plan to me."

Her gaze went back to the computer screen and she frowned.

"Everything okay?"

"No."

"No?"

"I can't figure out this blasted program. I need to fax a form over to the hospital and I can't get it to send. It would be quicker to walk it over."

Sloan walked over to her desk, bent down to glance at her computer screen, quickly spotting what she was doing wrong. "May I?"

"Be my guest." She pushed the computer mouse toward him. "Any moment now the system is probably going to crash thanks to my many failed attempts as there's no telling what I'm actually doing with all the clicking I'm doing."

"Just because you've faxed all our patients' records to Channel Four news doesn't mean our system is going to crash."

Her eyes widened. "I didn't."

He grinned. "You're right. You didn't."

"You're not a very nice man, Sloan Trenton. Here I am, trying to work my way through this crazy computer system and not bother anyone unnecessarily, and you give me a heart attack that I've sent confidential files to the local news station."

"You didn't believe me for a single second," he accused, knowing his words to be the truth.

A small smile played on her lips. "Well, maybe a single second."

Trying not to label the way his blood hammered through his vessels at her partial smile, Sloan clicked through the steps that would send Cara's fax. He also tried not to let the fact that he stood so close to where she sat distract him from his task. But she smelled good. And he'd bet that if he reached out and ran his fingers into that silky red hair she'd feel just as good. And her lips... He remembered all too well how those had felt. He hit the last button, watched the screen confirm that her fax had been sent properly then he straightened before her nearness cost him his mind.

"Thank you," Cara said immediately, glancing up at him from her chair. Her big blue-green eyes met his, locked for a few brief seconds and flickered with something he couldn't read. Her lips parted and then she shook her head very slightly and glanced back at the computer screen. "I'd have eventually figured the fax out, but having watched you send this will definitely make it easier next time."

Next time. Because she was going to be here for six months. Six months and then she'd leave, never to return to Bloomberg because she hated the town he loved. Preston's note flashed in front of his eyes and weighed heavily on his heart. Leave it to Preston to ask for the impossible, knowing Sloan would give it his all to make the man's dying request happen.

Never had he had anyone in his life ask so much of him; never had he had anyone put so much faith in him as Preston had. His last foster parents during high school had been kind to him, and the man, being a family physician, had lived the life Sloan had quickly realized he wanted—to serve others, to be a part of a tight-knit community and family, to make a difference in people's lives, to matter. That foster father had set Sloan on the course to becoming a doctor, but his relationship with him hadn't compared to the bond he'd formed with Preston. Even if he didn't one hundred percent agree with what Preston had requested, he had to do his best.

"For the record, we're all here to help you, Cara." They were. Everyone in the office was excited she was there. Not only because she was Preston's daughter but because he and Casey were in patient overload. So much so they'd already started looking for another nurse practitioner or physician's assistant. He supposed he should start putting out feelers for another physician as well for when Cara left. A pang shot through his chest, but he ignored it.

"We want to help you so, anything you can't figure out, ask. That way we know you're human, just like the rest of us."

She stared at the computer monitor as if it held the code to all life. "I'm all too human."

"Not everyone has climbed Everest or jumped out of a perfectly good airplane."

Both their gazes went to the smiling photos on the office wall.

"I should take those down, but I can't bring myself to change the way he has anything."

Sloan shrugged. "I don't think you should change them. I like the pictures."

"But they're all of me."

Yeah, there was that. He didn't know how to respond because what could he say? That one of the things he'd enjoyed most about Preston's office was the photos of his daughter? How could he possibly explain that to her? Or to himself, for that matter?

"Like I said, not everyone has done the things you've done or been to the places you have."

"Not in this town. In Bloomberg, everyone seems to think the world ends just outside the county lines."

Knowing he'd stayed in her office longer than he already should have, Sloan moved toward the door, pausing to lean against the frame. Surprised that she'd followed him to the doorway, he met her vivid blue gaze. "For them, perhaps it does."

Her gaze narrowed, but for once she didn't look away. "What do you mean?" she practically growled at him.

Apparently, he'd pushed a sensitive button or two. He'd need to tread cautiously or their truce would likely be a thing of the past. "For many of the people who live here there's no reason to go beyond the county lines because everything they love is right here in Bloomberg. Why go anywhere else?"

"Ugh, you sound like my father."

"I take that as a compliment."

Her lower lip disappeared between perfect white teeth and her shoulders lost their stiff edge. When her gaze met his, her eyes were clouded with inner turmoil. "It wasn't really meant to be a compliment."

Sloan battled some inner turmoil of his own, all of which was triggered by the way he reacted to everything about her. He shouldn't like her, but he did. He shouldn't want her, but he did.

The crazy thing was, as much as she'd tenaciously

deny it, he knew Cara fought the same inner battles. Not just because of her sleepy admission about finding him hot but because he saw it in her eyes.

Six months. Then she'd leave. Except he was supposed to convince her that Bloomberg was the place she wanted to spend the rest of her life.

Preston should not have put them in this situation, but he had.

Sloan reached out, brushed a hair away from her face and smiled despite his doubts. Surprisingly, she didn't pull away from his touch. "I know, Cara. I know."

Cara might not want to like Sloan, but the blasted man was growing on her. How could he not, with his constant smiles and teasing? Not just to her, but with everyone he came in contact with. Their coworkers, their patients, the hospital employees. Sloan was the most positive person she'd ever met. Just like her father, he gave his all to his patients.

After working with him for just a week, she understood why everyone said he was like Preston. The man woke up thinking about medicine, worked medicine wholeheartedly all day and, no doubt, went to bed thinking about medicine.

Case in point: his current text. She stared at her phone and read his message again, then typed a note back.

No problem. I will round on her in the morning and make sure another chest X-ray gets done.

Thanks. I'll be at the nursing home until about nine.

She'd noticed his schedule for the following day had been blocked for nursing-home rounds. Not that she'd

been looking at his schedule, just glancing at her own
to see how her morning appointments looked, to see
how many of the names she recognized.

You want to go with me to the nursing home? I can in-
troduce you to the staff and to our patients there so
you can take over rounding on Preston's patients. If
that's what you want to do.

Truly, Sloan had been gracious to her, had gone
above and beyond to make sure her transition into Conner Medical Clinic went smoothly. Because of him, because of their truce, the transition had been smooth.

She wasn't nearly as miserable as she'd anticipated.

Then again, she wasn't a young girl vying for her
father's attention while he was too busy caring for the
town's ailments. This time she stood in her father's
shoes and was the one caring for the townspeople.

Lord, how she missed him. In his house. In his clinic.
In his office. Everywhere, he remained. Everywhere
was his domain and she was just a secondary player.

Even with Sloan because she was positive that his
kindness to her was due to his respect for her father.

I could round earlier than usual and meet you at the
nursing home when I finish.

That works. See you in the morning, sunshine.

She wrinkled her nose at the nickname he'd given her
that first day when they'd been rounding at the hospital
and that seemed to have stuck. She didn't like it, was
pretty sure he was mocking her sour disposition about
being in Gloomberg, but whatever.

She didn't answer his text, just slid her phone into her pocket and paced across the living-room floor, wondering at the unease that tugged at her very soul.

She'd been in the house for a week.

Her childhood home. Yet she didn't feel at home here. Not really, because something was missing.

Someone was missing.

Although she knew it had been wrong of her father to have manipulated her so, she also knew that if she hadn't done as he wished, she'd regret not having done so for the rest of her life. Six months wasn't such a long time.

So why did the prospect of six months in Gloomberg feel like a nightmarish eternity looming before her?

She walked to her father's closed bedroom door, ran her fingers over the smooth wooden door. She'd not been able to go into his room yet. Silly of her, but she just couldn't. She'd asked Mrs. Johnson, who'd cleaned her father's house for years, not to go into the room, either.

Cara would go when she was ready, but that wasn't tonight.

"You're bright and early, sunshine."

Cara bristled at the nickname. She so wasn't a nickname kind of girl. "The name is Cara."

"Ah, well, that's an improvement, too, as I was beginning to think you just wanted me to call you Dr. Conner, but, then, that makes me feel as if I'm talking about Preston."

Cara flinched at the mention of her father. She couldn't help herself. She'd cried a big portion of the night as she'd replayed her father's visit to New York, as she tried to look for clues as to why he'd made the decisions he had. Then again, why question what she knew?

She'd been a disappointment to her father. He'd always wanted a son. She'd even overheard an argument between her parents once where Preston had even said as much to her mother.

As if he'd realized his gaff, Sloan grabbed her elbow and guided her toward the nursing home.

"I'm not a little old lady who needs help to cross the street."

"Seriously?" He made a pretense of visually perusing her spine. "I kind of thought you were."

She narrowed her gaze.

"Because I'm pretty sure you're so old that you've forgotten the truce we agreed to."

"I haven't forgotten."

"Just decided not to honor it today, because you feel particularly prickly?"

Grr. She hated it when he was right. "This is me during a truce."

"Then may we never be at odds."

She stopped walking just outside the nursing-home entrance and stared at him. "Make no mistake, Sloan. We are at odds. We've just called a temporary truce."

"A six-month one?"

She pushed the closest double glass door open and walked into the building, calling over her shoulder, "If you're lucky."

"And I behave?"

"Something like that."

"This one never behaves," a petite blonde nurse interrupted as they entered the nursing home. As casually as if touching him was no big deal, the woman wrapped her arms around Sloan and gave him a quick hug. "Thanks for the other night when I called you."

Sloan shrugged as if it were no big deal. "No problem."

Why had the woman called him? Personal or professional? What did it matter? What Sloan did outside work wasn't any of her business.

Even if she had spent the night in his arms a month ago and thought about him pretty much nonstop since. She squeezed her eyes shut and forced that memory from her mind. No way did she want that bogging her down today when so much of the night had been spent reminiscing about her father. When she had slept, she'd woken from dreams of the morning she'd woken in Sloan's arms. She'd been grumpy ever since.

"I'm glad you're here," the blonde nurse continued, walking down the hallway with them toward the east wing. "Ms. Campbell is coughing up some nasty green stuff this morning. I want you to listen to her lungs. I heard a few rhonchi in the left lower lobe, but would like your opinion."

"Sure thing. Lilly, do you know Dr. Conner?" He paused, then began again. "Dr. Cara Conner? She's working at the clinic and will be taking over her father's patients."

"You're Dr. Conner's daughter? Wow. I heard you were here, but I didn't realize you were so gorgeous."

"She is, isn't she?" Sloan agreed, grinning as Cara's cheeks flamed.

Cara thanked the woman, then turned all business without any further acknowledgement of her compliment. "Is Ms. Campbell one of my father's patients?"

Sloan answered for the nurse. "She is. Her daughter had her transferred from Mobile about a year ago when she became unhappy with the care she was receiving at a facility there. She's done well overall, but suffers from congestive heart failure and chronic obstructive pulmonary disease thanks to a lifelong smoking habit. Apparently, she didn't quit until she had the stroke that put her in the Mobile nursing home."

"Actually, we've caught her smoking in her bathroom a couple of times when she's convinced people to sneak her one or bummed one off of visitors who smoke," Lilly added, shaking her head in wry amusement. She met Cara's gaze and gave a friendly smile. "She's a handful, but we all adore her because she's so full of spunk."

"Yeah, yeah," Sloan said, rolling his eyes. "Tell her the real reason y'all adore her."

Eyes sparkling, Lilly laughed. "Ms. Campbell has decided that she's going to marry Sloan and is quite persistent in her pursuit of him. She believes he's into older women. Wouldn't surprise me in the slightest if she's faking the cough just so I'd have to call Sloan, except I hear the rhonchi."

Not surprised one bit that women of all ages found Sloan appealing, Cara arched her brow. "Interesting. How old is this Ms. Campbell?"

"Eighty," Lilly answered. "She was always happy seeing your father, but since Sloan checked her the first time, she's come up with a dozen ailments so I have to call him over."

"Is she who we are here to round on today?" she asked the pleasant nurse, who she just might like if not for that hug. Then again, she had no right not to like a woman just because she hugged Sloan and thanked him "for the other night."

She winced. Whether she should care or not, she did.

Whether that should influence how she felt about the nurse or not, it did.

"No," the woman answered, oblivious to the war Cara waged inside herself. "We have a list of patients to see today to update their chart orders, etcetera, but we will go in to check her, too."

"Awesome. I can't wait to meet her."

"And so you shall," Sloan said, eyeing her oddly, as if he could read her mind.

Thank God he couldn't really because the way he affected her confused her enough for both of them. No need to drag him into the chaos.

Sloan was wonderful with the older woman who suffered from mild dementia. He took everything the woman threw at him in his stride. From her suggestive comments to her marriage proposal. He remained all smiles and although he teased the woman back, he never lost his professional edge.

"Now, Ms. Campbell, you know I can't marry you. I'm a confirmed bachelor."

"Marry me and you will be confirmed my husband," the older woman countered, then sputtered with a coughing spell.

"You know it is a violation of doctor-patient relationship for me to marry you. We'll just have to settle with being friends," he told her between listening to her chest with his stethoscope.

"I can find a new doctor." She tapped Sloan's shoulder then pointed an arthritic finger at Cara. "She can be my doctor."

"Actually," he said, straightening to meet Cara's gaze, "she's my partner and is going to help take care of you, too."

His words didn't faze Cara. Really they didn't. That was only a flutter of gas causing her chest to feel funny. She wanted to correct him and say she wasn't his partner, just a temporary stand-in until the required time had passed, but Lilly and the patient shouldn't be privy to that conversation.

"If I had a husband I wouldn't need some woman to take care of me," the woman intoned with a loud sigh that started another coughing fit.

"Perhaps not, but Dr. Conner is an excellent physician and will be taking over her father's patients."

The woman frowned. "Who was her father?"

"Your former doctor. Dr. Conner."

"I don't know a Dr. Conner."

"He was your doctor for the past year," Sloan reminded.

The woman shook her head. "No, you are my doctor. I don't know a Dr. Conner."

Sloan gave Cara an apologetic glance. "Actually, this is Dr. Cara Conner. Her father was Dr. Preston Conner."

The woman didn't look convinced. "Where is he?"

"He died last month."

"That's sad," the woman said in a voice that truly conveyed the emotion. She turned earnest blue eyes toward Sloan. "We better hurry up and elope before you die. You're not getting any younger, you know."

"Now, you know, you're only as old as you feel, so I think I've got that one covered."

"Elope with me and I'll die a happy young woman."

"You're a mess," he advised, laughing, then pressed on her abdomen, checking all four quadrants.

The woman's gaze settled on Cara again. "Is she your girlfriend?"

Cara's cheeks burned but Sloan just smiled and continued to check the older woman.

"She's my partner," he repeated. "Dr. Cara Conner."

"That's a pretty name."

"Yes, it is. A pretty name for a pretty woman."

"I don't like her if she's your girlfriend."

"She's not my girlfriend. You've not been paying attention," Sloan tutted while checking pulses in her feet. "I don't have a girlfriend. I'm a confirmed bachelor."

"Much to all Bloomberg's females' broken hearts," Lilly added from behind them. "My theory is that there's already someone special in his life that he's just not told us about."

Laughing, Sloan shook his head. "Don't go starting rumors. The last thing I need is a bunch of matchmaking mommas trying to mend my broken heart."

Lilly's brow lifted and she showed genuine interest. "So you admit there is a broken heart?"

"Not really, but it sounded a good excuse for why I choose to be alone. Now, let me give you some verbal orders on our girl here."

Later, when they were walking out to the parking lot, Cara turned to him. "Why do you choose to be alone?"

Obviously caught off guard by her question, Sloan stopped walking. "Who says I choose to be alone?"

"You did in the patient room when Lilly said—"

"Lilly and nursing-home patients aren't privy to my personal life. I date, Cara. Not recently, because I've been so busy, but I'm not a monk and neither do I want to spend the rest of my life alone. I want a wife and kids, but not until it's with the right woman."

"Oh." Heat infused Cara's face as she realized that she was attempting to invade his personal space herself. "I shouldn't have pried."

"Why did you?"

Good question and one she wasn't sure of the answer to.

"I was just curious."

"You know what they say about being curious?"

She gave him a blank look.

"Curiosity killed the cat."

"Good thing I'm not a cat, then," she countered, then left him to stare after her while she hightailed it to her car and away from their conversation.

CHAPTER SEVEN

"HEY, BATTER—BATTER, SWING!" a teammate called out, as Sloan eyed the next batter stepping up to the plate.

His catcher stuck two fingers down, indicating the pitch she wanted him to throw. He shook his head.

Her gaze narrowed and she made another hand signal. He shook his head again. The catcher's mask failed to hide the displeasure twisting her lovely mouth. Anger flashed in her blue-green eyes then she gave another signal.

He nodded. Not because of the passionate spark in her eyes but because it was the pitch he'd intended to throw all along. Sloan had pitched against Robert Jenson before. The emergency-room doctor would tear up the fastball Cara had originally suggested, but the man couldn't hit Sloan's curve ball.

The man looked back at Cara, winked at her, then assumed the batter's stance.

Sloan didn't have to be a genius to know the emotion rocking through him was pure green jealousy at that wink and the smile Cara gave back to Robert. It was. The kind that made him want to scream and yell and beat on his chest and tell the man to leave her alone. She was his.

Only Cara wasn't his.

Sure, four months had gone by since she'd moved back to Bloomberg and stepped into her father's shoes. She'd maintained their truce. But that's as far as it went. On the surface she was polite and professional to him, but that's where she kept things. On the surface. She wouldn't let her guard down for one minute to actually get to know him or to let him in.

Was that what he still wanted? After months of them walking on eggshells? For Preston's snippy, snappy daughter to let him in?

Hell. It was.

For four months he'd been telling himself he was being cordial to her for Preston's sake, for the sake of the clinic and their patients, for his own sake because life was simpler if they got along for the time she was in Bloomberg.

Truth was, he was as fascinated by her as he'd ever been. More so.

Sloan twisted his arm around and flung the ball toward Cara's waiting glove.

Not as a curve, but a fastball. Not what he'd intended. Not what she'd been expecting.

Luckily, Robert must have been as distracted by that smiled response to his wink as Sloan had been because he swung half a second too late and the ball sailed by and went straight into Cara's waiting glove.

"Strike one," the umpire called out.

Cara's brow lifted in surprise as she stood and tossed the ball back to him for the next pitch.

Yeah, he'd said he wasn't going to throw a fast pitch. He knew. He needed to get his head in the game and off his pretty redheaded catcher.

Only she said something to the batter and the man's

face lit up like a Roman candle, his smile as wide as any Sloan had ever seen.

Was Cara flirting? For that matter, she could be dating Jenson. Sloan didn't know what she did, where she went, on her off-call weekends. Was she spending them with Jenson or some other man?

Sloan threw the ball. He couldn't say it was the worst pitch he'd ever thrown, but it sailed over to the right of the plate.

"Ball," the umpire called.

Cara gave him a "what's up" look and tossed the ball back his way.

"Hey, batter, batter," teammates and those sitting in the stands at the hospital charity softball game chanted.

Sloan threw another two pitches and the umpire repeated his calls. Ball. Ball. Not good.

He finally managed a decent curve ball with his next pitch. Robert swung and missed.

"Strike two!" the umpire shouted as he jerked his elbow back, indicating the call. "Full count."

Yeah, Sloan knew. He really didn't want the doctor to get onto base. It was the fourth inning and his team was up by two runs. But Becky Wisdom from Accounting had gotten a decent single and was just waiting to take off toward second if Robert nailed one.

Robert turned, said something to Cara that made her laugh. The sound was both magical and irritating. Magical in that he rarely heard her laugh, although it did seem to be happening more and more frequently as she became closer to the women who worked in the office. Irritating because another man had triggered the sound.

Sloan hiked his leg, reared back and threw the ball for all he had.

Robert got a piece of the ball, but it fouled out to the right. The first baseman caught it for an easy out.

Robert gave a disgusted shake of his head, but whatever Cara said to him made him grin and nod his head. Urgh. She was flirting. With the opposing team.

Who were really only their coworkers.

As Robert left the field and the next batter settled in by the plate, Sloan racked his brain, trying to recall just how much time Cara spent with Robert. Who was he kidding? He had no idea what she did in her spare time although she might smile and flirt with Robert, she still only spoke with *him* when it was absolutely necessary. She was polite, friendly enough at the clinic, and that was it. No such smiles for him.

And definitely no flirting.

He gripped the softball so tightly he was surprised the ball wasn't crushed. He took a couple of deep breaths, reminded himself that what Cara did, who she talked to or flirted with didn't matter, and he gave a nice normal slow pitch of the ball to one of the phlebotomists.

The guy hit the ball midfield, made it to second and brought Becky all the way around to third base.

Cara motioned that she wanted to meet with him and made her way to the pitcher's mound.

"What's up?"

"You tell me."

"Huh?" She looked as confused as he felt.

"You're flirting with the players," he accused, daring her to deny his claim.

"What?"

"I saw the way you and Robert were carrying on." Did his disgust ooze from his words?

"Um, what does that have to do with your pitching?"

Good question. This woman tore him into bits. He sure couldn't tell her the truth.

But the truth must have been all over his face because her eyes widened. "You're jealous."

He was tired of being treated like the enemy. He hadn't had a thing to do with the decisions Preston had made. All he'd done was love the man and been fascinated by his daughter. How dared she hold that against him? How dared she treat him like he had the bubonic plague while she made googly eyes at other men?

He shrugged and held her gaze. "What if I am?"

What, indeed? Cara thought, staring at Sloan in surprise. Sure, he'd been nice to her, more so than she deserved, from the moment she'd arrived in Bloomsberg. But what she was seeing on his face wasn't friendliness or kindness. It was possessiveness.

Which was ridiculous. Why would he be possessive of her? Jealous about her?

Only she knew.

Hadn't she known from the beginning that there was something different about him? Something that sparked between them every time he was near? Only she had so much animosity toward him that she'd pushed aside the chemistry and labeled the emotions brewing inside her as disgust or anger.

Or tried to. For four months she'd been trying to convince herself, trying to stay away from him except when absolutely necessary. Longer than that, really. From that first night.

Only in this heated moment there was no labeling the way Sloan was looking at her and the way her body was reacting as anger.

He was jealous that he thought she was flirting with another man.

Most surprising of all, she liked that flare of passion, that possessiveness in his eyes.

That terrified her, made her want to lash out, made her want to protect herself from possible heartache.

"Get your act together, Sloan," she growled, eyes narrowed, hands on her hips. "We have a game to finish and I don't intend to lose because your head is elsewhere."

Only it was her head that wasn't in the rest of the game.

Cara had always excelled in sports, had always loved the physical demands put on her body. But for the next three innings she couldn't keep her focus on anything other than her pitcher.

With every pitch her eyes met his and when he released the ball and it sailed into her waiting glove it was as if he reached out and touched her. Crazy. An opposing team batter stood between them. Twenty feet lay between them. A crowd of people was around them. Yet they were the only two players. His release and her catch became more and more sensual with each throw.

She felt it. The darkness in his eyes said he felt it.

"Strike three. You're out," the umpire told the batter.

Cara straightened and stretched her legs. She'd worked out and run regularly in New York and had kept up the habit while in Bloomberg, but it had been quite a few years since she'd spent any time in a catcher's squat. Her knees and calves were protesting the seven innings she'd spent in the position.

They had one at bat left.

The game was tied six to six.

Robert Jenson had taken over the pitcher's mound for his team and was throwing some warm-up pitches.

First up to bat for their team was a guy from Finance, a nurse from the medical floor, and then they'd be at the top of their batting line-up again. Sloan and then Cara.

Finance guy struck out in three pitches. Cara held her breath while the nurse stood straight up over the plate, closed her eyes and swung half a mile too late for the ball. There was a reason Gail was their last batter. Sweet, an amazing nurse, but claimed to have never held a bat prior to today's game.

"Bend your body. Swing a little quicker. Keep your eyes open. You've got this," she said, offering encouragement.

Cara had always loved sports. During her long, lonely hours growing up, she'd lost herself as part of whichever team she'd played for. Softball, soccer, basketball, track, golf, tennis, swimming—the sport hadn't mattered. Just that she'd pushed her body to the max and that she'd done her team—and her father—proud. Some kids acted out to try to get their parents' attention. She'd tried to excel at everything instead. Still, it hadn't been good enough to keep her father's attention for more than a few seconds. There had always been another patient, someone who had needed him more than his daughter.

She huffed out a deep sigh, realized she'd totally missed the pitch and Gail's failed attempt to make contact.

"Strike two," the umpire called.

Cara let her gaze leave Gail and go to the man standing in the warm-up spot. A man who had held her father's attention and had been good enough in his eyes.

He was good enough in her eyes.

Um, no! she corrected her brain, which was obviously suffering from heat stroke—and it wasn't even that hot out here.

Just because Sloan's biceps bulged beneath his neon-green and blue T-shirt did not mean he was good enough in her eyes. Just because his baseball pants clung to his narrow hips and muscular thighs did not mean he was good enough in her eyes. Just because there had been some kind of wild sparks passing between them in that last inning when he'd been tossing the ball into her glove time and again did not mean a thing.

Because she was not a superficial kind of girl. Yes, he was gorgeous. No matter how much she wanted to deny that, she couldn't. His coppery eyes, dark hair, and quick grin should be gracing the pages of a magazine. But she so wasn't interested in a man who had achieved what she'd never been able to attain.

Not that she was interested in Sloan. She wasn't. What would be the point? She was big city. He was country.

As if he sensed she was checking him out, he turned, his gaze connecting with hers. That zap burned straight through her. It wasn't his looks or his brain or even his body that got to her. It was exactly what was happening this second. This annoying total-body meltdown that happened when he looked into her eyes and she could see that he wanted her.

Sloan wanted her.

Maybe he had from the beginning.

Maybe that was why he'd automatically assumed she'd been asking him to stay the night with her for sex the night he'd driven her home from the funeral parlor.

Maybe that was why she should ask him to stay the night for sex.

Um, no!

She was not asking Sloan over for sex. What would she say? *Hey, Sloan. I resent that my father thought you hung the moon. It irks me that he forced me to have to work side by side with you to get to keep my mother's things. But, hey, I think you are hot, I haven't had sex in eons and I'd like you to rock my world tonight.*

He would rock her world. She was sure of it. Sure he would rock her world in ways that her world had never been rocked because although she had enjoyed her sex life with John well enough she couldn't say there had been any world rocking going on. But with Sloan…with Sloan, no doubt he'd be as perfect at evoking every drop of passion from her as he was at every other blasted thing.

She *so-o-o-o* didn't like him. Detested him.

Wanted him.

Cara gulped. Sloan's brow rose. She shook her head.

To what exactly she wasn't sure, but maybe Sloan knew because his brow arched even higher. Then he grinned. Not an amused grin but an I-have-you-now grin. Surely the man didn't also list mind-reading skills on his already impressive résumé? Urgh. He was way too perfect.

"Two down. Only one to go," one of their opposing teammates called out, calling Cara's attention back to the game.

Gail had struck out.

Next up to bat was Sloan. No doubt he'd hit a home run and win the game and be the hero of the day. He was that kind of guy. A hero in everyone's eyes but hers. Or at the minimum he'd get on base and then it would be her turn to either keep things going or end the inning. Once upon a time she'd have not even questioned which.

But until today she hadn't held a bat in quite a few years herself. Funny, she'd pretty much given up team sports at some point during medical school. She took a deep breath and replaced Sloan in the next batter-up spot. She'd missed this.

Not Bloomberg, but this being a part of a team, a part of something where people depended on each other and interacted with each other. She'd been part of the emergency room team at the hospital where she'd worked and yet there was a difference. An indifference to each other as coworkers and individuals.

Not here. Not in Bloomberg.

Sloan held the bat high, poised for the pitch, and then the ball sailed towards him. He gave it a good, solid hit into the outfield and made it to third base just as the ball came sailing into the catcher's glove at home plate.

Cara stepped into the batter box. She'd either be the belle of the ball or the disappointment.

Robert smiled at her as he prepped to pitch. Maybe she should accept his invitation of a date. He was a good-looking man, fun, wasn't her father's golden boy, and wasn't looking for a committed relationship any more than she was.

But she wasn't looking for a noncommitted relationship, either. Only Sloan had her thinking about physical needs and that had her body all stirred up. She didn't want to date. She wanted…

Sloan.

She swung the bat as hard as she could and made contact with the ball. Hard contact that ripped through her body. It felt good.

She took off toward first as fast as she could. She'd just rounded first and was headed toward second when cheers went up from the stands. Sloan had made it home.

Whether she ran or walked the rest of the way didn't matter. They'd won the game.

Everyone was gathered around Sloan and high-fiving him when Cara tapped her foot on home.

"Great job, Cara!" Julie praised her, as another teammate slapped Cara on the back and said similar words. High fives and back slaps abounded. Another chest bumped her and, laughing, Cara turned toward the player who'd just stepped up to her, ready to accept more congratulations. Wow. She'd forgotten just how much fun being a part of a team was.

The person waiting wrapped his arms around her and spun her around, increasing her laughter and stirring a whole new type of excitement. Sloan. He came to a stop and slowly released her. She just as slowly slid down his body to stand close to him. So close their bodies still touched.

Her gaze met his and her laughter faded.

"Nice hit," he said, his coppery eyes not leaving her face.

"Thank you," she managed, despite the lump in her throat. Why, oh, why was she thinking about how much she'd like to lick him? He was hot and sweaty and she didn't like him. Licking wasn't an option.

Yet she wanted her mouth on his throat. Wanted her tongue tracing over the pulse that beat wildly at his nape. Wanted her arms back around his neck and her body pressed up against the hard planes of his chest. She might as well just face the truth. Whether she liked him or not, she wanted Sloan.

"Um," she gulped, knowing she had to do something, to say something. "You run good."

You run good? Really? Could she have found more stupid-sounding words to say?

His eyes sparkled like molten copper and his mouth curved into the sexiest smile she'd ever seen. "Thanks for noticing."

Not that she had. She'd had her focus on her own run and he knew that. Which was why he was smiling.

She stepped back from him, turned to the person next to her and started talking enthusiastically about the game. With words that weren't quite so ridiculous as *you run good*.

Anything to break the connection between her and Sloan.

The following night, Sloan parked his car in the doctors' parking lot and jogged into the hospital. There had been a multicar crash that had resulted in multiple injuries, some serious. One had been a car full of local teenagers on their way back from a weekend in Pensacola. Jenson was in the emergency room, but when the call about the crash had come in to get the emergency room ready for multiple victims, Sloan had been called in to assist as the rural hospital emergency room wasn't equipped for the number of victims on their way.

He'd expected utter chaos when he entered the emergency department. What he hadn't expected was to see Jenson and Cara laughing as they set up a patient area.

Jenson said something. Cara laughed and nudged his shoulder with her own. Sloan's lungs quit working and his head spun from lack of oxygen.

The vision of them, the camaraderie, the lack of

tension irritated him. Why could she look at Jenson and smile freely but keep up all her walls with *him*?

Why was he thinking about that when there were lives to be saved? He needed to get scrubbed and help get the emergency room ready for the pending onslaught.

Working multicar crashes was nothing new for Cara. Having worked in the emergency room in Manhattan, she was used to seeing all different types of trauma. So why taking care of a car full of teenagers, an elderly couple and a family of four had her reeling, she wasn't sure.

This was her specialty. What she did best. She loved ER work. It's what she planned to return to when her six-month Gloomberg stint finished.

She sent a kid with suspected internal injuries to get a computerized tomography test of his chest and abdomen, while another got an MRI of his head. The elderly couple were being x-rayed.

As the actual physician working the emergency room, Dr. Jenson was overseeing the driver of the teenagers' car. The kid's consciousness was coming and going. He had multiple internal injuries, including a crushed pelvis. Robert had called to have him airlifted to a trauma hospital in Pensacola and was trying to keep him alive and stable until the helicopter arrived.

Sloan worked on the father of the family of four. The man had multiple facial lacerations and a fractured humerus. The youngest of the family was a one-year-old who had thankfully been in her car seat and had avoided any serious injuries. The little girl sobbed loudly as she clung to her mother. The mother had several lacerations that were going to require suturing, but currently Cara was working on a three-year-old little girl who had a cut that ran down her forehead and into her eyebrow and other bits of embedded glass on her forehead.

Cara had mildly sedated the child, had her restrained in a bed sheet, and worked tediously to remove the bits of broken glass from her forehead in the area of the main cut, which still bled quite profusely.

She rinsed the open area with saline then closed the skin with a special skin glue. By the time she'd finished cleaning up the three-year-old's forehead and turned her over to the nurse who had assisted with the procedure, the girl's one-year-old sister had given up sobbing and slept in her mother's arms.

"Is Adelaine going to be okay? She was bleeding so much. I was so scared," the woman said, lifting her own bandage away from her forehead and looking at the blood-saturated gauze.

"The best we can tell. She doesn't have any major internal injuries. She has a few nasty cuts on her face that I've done my best to remove the glass from and close, but oftentimes bits of glass will work their way out for months after an accident." Cara washed her hands and put on a fresh pair of latex-free gloves. "Now, let's take a look at getting you closed up."

Cara quickly cleaned the wound and stitched the area closed with the tiniest thread the emergency room offered.

"That's a really nice job."

"Thank you." Cara tied off the last suture and tried to pretend she wasn't startled to see Sloan standing next to her or that his praise didn't please her.

"I've admitted your husband for overnight observation," he explained to the woman. "Mostly so we can keep an eye on him."

A fresh wave of panic crossed the woman's face. "Is he okay?"

"I believe he's going to be fine. His right humerus is broken, probably from when the airbag went off. It saved his life but broke his arm in the process. He's bruised, but I don't find any evidence of internal bleeding or organ damage. I just want a close eye kept on him tonight."

"Thank God." The woman breathed a sigh of relief.

Code blue. Code blue. Radiology.

Sloan and Cara both looked at each other. Not good.

Dr. Jenson was still tied up with the teen driver so Sloan and Cara took off for the radiology department.

A nurse joined them, pushing the crash cart.

One of the teens getting imaging had stopped breathing. A nurse who'd been with the teen was performing CPR, but to no avail.

"Multiple internal injuries with head trauma," Sloan said, as they set up the defibrillator and Cara prepped the patient for the electrical shock, checking telemetry. He gave the nurse an order to inject epinephrine and then told everyone to stand clear.

"Now," he said, and Cara pushed the button that would deliver the surge of electrical stimulation to the patient's heart. Nothing.

The ventilator breathed for the patient, providing a steady flow of oxygen, but there was still no heartbeat. Cara gave a set of compressions while the defibrillator reset. Still nothing. They delivered another jolt of electricity. Nothing.

They repeated the process but couldn't get a heartbeat started on the teen. The nurse with them let out a soft cry. "I hate this."

Cara nodded. So did she. That had been the one part

of the emergency department she'd never liked. Death. In Manhattan it had been unfamiliar faces, unfamiliar names she'd dealt with. Here, in Bloomberg, she knew this teen's family, knew the girl's father worked at a bank as a loan officer, knew the girl's mother had played on the high school basketball team a decade or so before Cara had.

She wouldn't be delivering bad news to strangers. She'd be delivering bad news to people she knew. That was the difference between big-city medicine and Bloomberg.

Letting out a pained sigh of his own, Sloan put his arm around the nurse's shoulder. "None of us do, but we did all we could." He hugged her, took a deep breath. "Is her family here?"

Cara felt relief start coursing through her. Sloan planned to talk to the family. She wouldn't have to be the bearer of such horrible news to the girl's parents.

The nurse nodded. "I was told they arrived not long after the ambulance showed up."

Sloan nodded, gave the woman another squeeze around the shoulders then met Cara's gaze. Such empathy and compassion showed there that Cara took a step back. Not that she didn't see Sloan's compassion for his patients on a daily basis at the clinic, but there was such deep sadness there that she ached for him.

"I'll go talk to them," she volunteered, her gaze not wavering from his.

To her surprise, he shook his head. "Jeff is my friend. He was one of the first people I met when I came to Bloomberg. I should be the one to tell him."

Cara wasn't sure she agreed with Sloan but he didn't give her a chance to argue, just turned and left the room.

Cara glanced around at the somber faces still present,

at the young, lifeless body. For all the good they'd done the other crash victims, they'd not been able to do enough for this young girl. Her heart ached at the lost dreams and hopes, at the sadness so many would feel at the loss.

She wasn't a cold doctor in New York, but she wasn't sure she'd ever considered the ripple effect of a loss of life quite so harshly as at this moment. Bloomberg had lost one of its own and the entire town would mourn.

Just as they'd all mourned the loss of her father.

Perhaps there was something to be said about small-town life but, regardless, more than ever Cara just wished she were far, far away.

CHAPTER EIGHT

IT WAS SEVERAL hours later before the emergency room calmed down enough that Sloan felt okay about leaving the hospital. He'd stayed until all transfers, admissions, and discharges had been made and the emergency room was back to doable for Dr. Jenson.

The medical evacuation helicopter had arrived for the teenage boy while Sloan had been talking to Jeff and his wife, Cindy. That had been a hellish conversation. The entire night had been hellish.

"Sloan?"

Surprised at the voice, he turned toward Cara. Her eyes were big, her face pale. She looked as tired as he felt.

"I thought you'd already left."

Because he had looked for her. Hopefully not too obviously, but he had looked and hadn't been able to find her.

She glanced toward where her car was parked a few spaces down from his Jeep. "I…I was waiting on you."

Perhaps he was so tired he was hallucinating, because surely she hadn't been sitting in her car, waiting for him to come out of the hospital. "Why?"

She bit her lower lip, shrugged, and looked as uncertain as he'd ever seen her look.

"I was worried about you," she said finally.

Yep, he was definitely hallucinating. "I'm okay."

"I could tell how upset you were about the Davis kid."

He nodded. What else could he do? The death of someone so young was such a waste, something he'd never understand. Jeff and Cindy's lives would never be the same. So many lives would never be the same after this tragedy of a car wreck that had involved so many from their community. And he prayed the airlifted boy would survive and the town wouldn't be facing an even worse tragedy.

"For whatever it's worth…" She looked pensive, as if she searched for the right words. She looked up at him with her big, clear blue-green eyes that, upon looking closer, weren't so clear but red-rimmed. "I'm sorry."

He studied her expression. She looked genuinely upset, genuinely concerned about him, and she'd been crying.

"You have nothing to be sorry for, Cara." He reached out and lifted her chin, stared into her sad eyes, thinking that a more beautiful woman had never existed than the one shooting awareness through his fingertips. "You were great in there." Lord, her skin was so soft, so delicate beneath his fingers, so very electrifying. "If I ever have to be intubated, I request you do it, by the way. You make that procedure look easy."

"I had lots of practice in New York." Closing her eyes, she shuddered and rubbed her hands over her arms. "I pray you never have to be intubated, Sloan. Never."

He really must be hallucinating because she seemed so lost, so different than who she normally was. The only other time he'd seen her look this fraught had been the night he'd carried her home from the funeral parlor.

A night that hadn't ended well when she'd woken the next morning and treated him as if he had the plague. The memory had left a bitter taste in his mouth and in his mind.

"Odd," he mused out loud, in protective defense mode. "I'd have guessed you'd like to see me gone."

Stepping back from him, she frowned. "That's a horrible thing to say."

Knowing she was right and that memory of the past had influenced his comment, guilt slammed him. "You're right. I shouldn't have said that."

Especially since she'd waited for him, sought him out to have a conversation. How often did that happen outside the office regarding a patient's care? Never.

"I'm the one who's sorry," he continued. Very sorry. "Guess I'm just tired. We'll just say that if I ever have to be sutured, you can do it. Those were some neat stitches you did tonight."

"Okay, deal. I hope you never need to be sutured, but if you do, I'm your girl." Her lower lip disappeared between her teeth then she sighed. "I'm tired, too. Exhausted." Rubbing her hands over her arms again, she glanced around the dimly lit private doctors' parking area. "I'm too wound up to go home to sleep, though."

He waited, not sure where she was going with her statement but determined not to jump to any conclusions. That tended to get him into trouble where she was concerned.

Her gaze cut back to him. "Do you think we could go somewhere?"

Sloan's breath caught. What exactly was she asking him? Because he was having a really hard time fighting those jumped-to conclusions when she looked at him the way she was looking at him. Eyes wide, lips parted, and her expression needy.

"It doesn't matter where. Anywhere is fine," she added, when he didn't respond immediately. Did she think he'd say no? That he could say no to her? He'd like to think he could, but she got to him. She'd always gotten to him. Could you fall for someone based on how another person talked about them? Based on the sparkle in their eyes in a photo? Lord, he was exhausted. Must be with as crazy as his thoughts were.

"It's after eleven on a Sunday night in Bloomberg. There's not a lot of options. There's only one place even open at this time of night."

"Then let's go there," she suggested quickly, sliding her hands into her scrub pockets and waiting for his answer almost anxiously.

"It's a drive-up fast-food place." What was he trying to do? Talk her out of spending time with him?

He should be talking her out of spending time with him.

Or should he? He didn't know anymore. She confused him.

Then there was Preston's will and last request...

That was a kicker of a dilemma that he still hadn't quite figured out how to deal with, how he even wanted to deal with it.

"I know. I used to live here, remember?" She gave him a tentative smile that shoved all thoughts of Preston's will and last request right out of his head.

"How could I forget?"

"We can take my car, if that's okay. Hop in."

Whatever she wanted was okay with Sloan. He was exhausted, but adrenaline that she wanted to spend time with him was taking over, erasing the fatigue from his body. Or maybe it was her half smile directed at him that had his blood hammering through his veins?

While they were driving toward the fast-food place, he studied her profile. She stared intently at the road as if she expected something terrible to happen to their car. That's when he realized just how much the wreck they'd worked had affected her.

"Don't watch me," she ordered, sounding as bossy as ever, but her shoulders sagged.

"Don't watch you drive or don't look at you in general?"

Her fingers gripped the steering wheel tightly. "Both."

Sloan's heart squeezed at the sight she made. So determined to be brave, so determined not to like him, and yet she'd waited. Why? Because she felt the connection between them that they'd been fighting for months?

Sloan was tired of fighting. Fighting her. Fighting the way he felt about her. Fighting his conflicting feelings over Preston's will and last request. He was tired of all of it.

"Hate to break it to you, sunshine, but there's not another thing in sight worth looking at except you."

"I don't like it when you call me that," she reminded him, not glancing his way and not addressing his compliment at all.

"Add it to my list of crimes."

"You don't have a list of crimes," she countered immediately.

"Sure I do." At her questioning glance his way he added, "Maybe not a written one, but you definitely have a mental list of all the reasons you don't like me."

Her grip tightened even more on the steering wheel, blanching her knuckles. "That's the problem."

"What?"

"I don't want to like you, Sloan."

"But?"

"But I can't seem to help myself," she said, so softly he had to mentally repeat her words to absorb them.

"Why is that a problem? I'm not your enemy, Cara."

"I think you are."

"Why would you think that? Because of your father's will? I had nothing to do with the changes he put into effect. I don't like them any more than you do."

"You have everything to gain by those changes." She hesitated just long enough that he wondered if he was wrong, if it wasn't really the will that was the problem.

"I lost more when your father died than any will can ever replace."

"He loved you." A rough sound escaped her lips that Sloan wasn't sure was a gasp or a sob.

"Yes," Sloan agreed, knowing Preston truly had cared for him. Then what Cara had said, how she'd said it, soaked in. "Your father loved you, too, Cara. More than life itself that man loved you."

She slowed the car then pulled into a vacant building parking lot and put the ignition into park. The street-light across the street and the dashboard lights lit the car just enough to illuminate her features.

"I know he loved me." She was definitely crying now, crying and trying to keep him from realizing that's what was happening. "In his own way."

"In every way." How could she doubt Preston's feelings for her? The man had thought she walked on water and shined brighter than any star in the sky.

"I was too much like my mother for him to understand me." She sucked in a little air and lifted her shoulders, her hands gripping the steering wheel, then sliding down them to rest in her lap.

Sloan ached to wrap his arms around her and comfort her. "Doesn't mean the man didn't love you with all his heart."

She gave a low laugh. "He wanted a boy."

What? He had never heard Preston say anything to that effect. But he hadn't known the man nearly as long as his daughter had. Perhaps Preston had said something at some point that made her believe that.

"Most men think they want a son, but it's their daughter who wraps them around her finger." He reached across the console and took her hand into his, stroked his fingers across hers, and was quite positive Cara could easily wrap him around her finger.

She stared down at their hands but didn't pull away from him. "My father wasn't the kind of man to be wrapped around anyone's finger."

"Perhaps not," he agreed, thinking of the powerful man Preston Conner had been, "but he adored you, Cara. You were what he was most proud of."

She shook her head. "I failed him." Her voice broke just a little and Sloan's heart squeezed a lot.

"You didn't," he said, knowing it was true. As much as Preston had wanted his daughter in Bloomberg, he'd been proud of her and her accomplishments. Sloan didn't doubt that for a second.

"You don't understand. He wanted me to move home and I refused."

"That was your right and definitely doesn't make you a failure," he assured her, wishing he had the right to lift her hand to his lips and press a kiss to her skin. Wishing he had the right to pull her to him and hold her close. He hadn't really thought about how the teen's death might trigger Cara's own grief over her father, but it had. Obviously, she was struggling and dealing with an emotional onslaught.

"If I'd known…"

"Hindsight is always twenty-twenty. Most all of us would do things differently if we knew what the future held."

She turned toward him, giving him a truly confused stare. "Why are you being so nice to me?"

If she weren't so serious, he could have laughed at her question. But she genuinely didn't understand. "Because, despite what you think, I'm not your enemy."

She sighed, leaning forward and putting her forehead against the steering wheel. "So you keep saying."

"Sunshine?"

"I ought not answer when you call me that," she admonished, a little of her usual spark coming through as she straightened back up in her seat.

"If you'd let me, I'd like to hold you."

She turned toward him, her forehead wrinkled. "Here? Now? In the car in a vacant parking lot?"

"Yes. Here. Now. In the car in a vacant parking lot. I feel as if I'm giving an answer through the words of a childhood story." He laughed, hoping her expression would also lighten. He couldn't bear the sadness in her eyes.

"Why would you want to hold me, Sloan?"

Why? He could tell her how seeing her tears touched places inside him he wasn't sure had ever been touched. He could tell her how he wanted to share her grief over a man they'd both loved. He could tell her how he craved to feel her body against his again, because holding her for that brief celebratory spin the day before had left him longing for much more. He could tell her how the night he had spent holding her haunted his dreams. He could. But he wouldn't, because what would be the point?

"Quit asking questions," he ordered instead, "and just say yes or no."

"Yes or no."

His lips twitched. "Smart-mouthed woman."

With that, Sloan didn't wait for permission, just leaned toward her, ran his fingers into her hair and gently tilted her face toward him. Her eyes caught the reflection of the streetlight, making them sparkle in the dimly lit car.

Her gaze held his, almost daring him to say more, to do more, to take what he wanted from her. Her lips parted, teasing him with the promise of entrance into that gorgeous mouth of hers. He wanted to taste her, longed to taste her. The morning he'd woken up with her in his arms seemed so long ago. Surely he'd dreamed the passion, the sweetness of her kisses?

He really needed to know.

He leaned toward her, his gaze zeroing in on his destination. "Such a beautiful, tempting mouth to hold such a sharp, sharp tongue."

Sloan was about to kiss her. Cara should stop him. Their emotions were just high from the emergency-room drama. At least, hers were. She knew that.

She also knew that she had been thinking about Sloan kissing her for the past four months. Longer.

From the morning she'd woken up to his body moving against hers, to his lips covering hers, she'd wanted more kisses, wanted his body against hers.

Yesterday, when he'd spun her around and let her glide down his body, every nerve ending in her body had been aware of him. She'd wanted to wrap her arms around his neck, mash her body against his and kiss him.

Kiss him and kiss him and kiss him until they'd both been breathless and clinging to each other the way they had that morning. More. Way beyond that. She wanted everything.

She wanted everything now.

Cara leaned forward and closed the gap between their mouths, pressing her lips to his.

Instant pleasure rewarded her action. Oh, how sweet Sloan's mouth was against hers. Hungry and passionate and demanding. Flutters shimmied in her belly. Warmth spread through her being. She scooted toward him, wishing the car didn't have bucket seats, wishing she could be as close to him as she wanted to be. Her fingers wound into his hair, almost painfully, she was sure, daring him to move away from her mouth. She needed his kisses. Needed what he was eliciting in her body. She needed to feel alive and Sloan made her feel more alive than she'd ever felt.

"Woman, you're killing me," he breathed against her lips.

"Me? How?" she asked, kissing him again, loving the taste of him, loving the strength she felt in his every touch.

"Because I want you, Cara, and five minutes from now you're going to realize who it is you're kissing and you're going to hate yourself for kissing me. Then I'm going to be the bad guy again."

He was right. "You're the bad guy right now."

Drawing a shaky breath, he pulled back from her, but she refused to loosen her grasp on his hair so he didn't go far. "I don't want you to stop kissing me. I want you to kiss me, Sloan. I desperately want you kissing me. Just don't stop and then I won't have regrets."

Then he was kissing her again. Over and over, demanding and yet tender. He kissed her with the passion she craved. He kissed her with reverence and yet masterfully. He kissed her even better than her memory had recalled.

Sloan kissed her and her crazy, unbalanced world slid into perfect harmony.

"I'd like to go to your place, but I'm not going to," Sloan told her much later, when they sat in her car back in the hospital parking lot. After their make-out session, she'd driven them back to the hospital parking lot rather than the now-closed drive-up restaurant.

"I didn't invite you to my place," she immediately reminded him.

He sighed. "You're right. You didn't. I shouldn't make assumptions where you are concerned. I know that."

"You shouldn't, but, to be fair, if I thought you'd say yes, I'd invite you, Sloan." Her gaze held his. "Because I'd be lying if I said that wasn't what I wanted."

Heaven help him. How was he supposed to do the right thing and not beg her to invite him when she'd admitted that she wanted him there?

"Don't say that."

"Why not? It's the truth."

"Because you don't understand how much willpower it requires for me to do the right thing where you're concerned."

"Not going to my place is the right thing?"

Earlier tonight he'd been her enemy in her eyes. She still claimed to see him that way. A relationship between them based on lust went against everything his head told him. "Yes, I believe it is."

She took a few moments to consider his comment. "Because of my father?"

An affair sure wouldn't win him any brownie points toward giving Preston what he wanted. "Because of a lot of reasons, but mainly because you see me as your enemy."

She didn't deny it, but offered, "You could show me all the reasons why I shouldn't see you that way."

He wanted to show her a lot of things, like how good it could be between them. Unfortunately, they wanted very different things in the long term and he was already so wrapped up in her that he wasn't sure he'd recover from an affair with Cara.

"Don't get me wrong," he admitted. "I'd like to do exactly that, but sex would only complicate things between us."

She leaned back in the driver's seat, put her hands on the steering wheel, stared straight ahead, then shocked him with what she said next. "Things are already complicated between us. We can both deny it, but we both know it's true. Besides, what's a little sex between enemies?"

Which was exactly why they shouldn't have sex.

"You aren't my enemy. Just as I'm not yours." He reached out, ran his finger across her cheek. "And, for the record, there wouldn't be a 'little sex' between you and I. If, and when, we take that step, it'll be big. Gigantic even."

"Sheesh. Men." She rolled her eyes. "I wasn't referring to your size."

"Neither was I, but in all regards sex between you and I would be huge." He let the last word roll off his tongue slowly, liking the way her eyes closed, her throat worked, and her fingers gripped the steering wheel tighter.

"But you aren't willing to go home with me tonight, are you?"

Blast Preston for the position he'd put them in with his crazy requests. Blast himself for caring about Cara and not wanting to take advantage of her current emotional state. Blast having scruples and not wanting to have sex with someone who regarded him as her enemy.

Sloan shook his head. "Not tonight. Too much has happened today. Our emotions are too raw. If you still want me in the light of day, we'll talk."

"Perhaps you misunderstand." She tapped her fingers against the steering wheel. "Talking isn't what I want."

He groaned. If his words had affected her body, hers had done so tenfold to his. Did she have any idea how difficult this was on him? How difficult pulling away from their heated kisses had been?

But the next time Cara spent the night in his arms he wouldn't have her telling him to get out when she woke up. The next time she'd spend the night with him willingly, with no regrets when morning came. The next time wouldn't be triggered by her not wanting to be alone in her house because she was grieving for her father.

There would be a next time. He believed that with all his being, which was what gave him the strength to lean forward, press a kiss to her cheek, and then open the car door. "Good night, Cara. I'll follow you home and make sure you get inside safely. Sweet dreams."

"Can you look over June Lucada's labs? She's on the phone, wanting her results," Amie informed Cara, poking her head into her office.

Rubbing her temple, hoping the throb there would ease, Cara fought a yawn. "Sure thing. Is it in my inbox?"

"Yep. It's there. You want me to have her hold or tell her we'll call her back in a few?"

"Have her hold, and I'll take a look now." Fighting another yawn, Cara opened her electronic inbox and reviewed the patient's labs. She picked up the phone and gave the woman the results and advised her to schedule a follow-up appointment to address her elevated cholesterol.

"How's your husband doing?" she asked, referring to the man she'd seen the previous week. "Is his big toe any better?"

While she listened to the woman explain how the man's gout had improved with the medication Cara had given him, Cara glanced up to see she was being watched by a tall, lean specimen of perfection leaning against her door frame.

Almost perfection, because, thanks to him, she was as exhausted this morning as she'd been when she'd crawled into bed. How had she been supposed to sleep after those heated kisses? Obviously she hadn't because all she'd done had been to lie in bed and think about him. That was, until she'd finally crawled out of bed, gone down the hallway and opened a closed wooden door. Her father's room. As much as it had ached to enter the room, it had been time. Past time. She supposed the girl's death had pushed her into the room. Or maybe entering the room, dealing with painful emotions, had been the only way to clear her mind of Sloan.

Either way, she hadn't slept and she hadn't been able to quit thinking about Sloan.

She'd kissed him last night. Kissed him over and

over. She'd run her fingers through those coal-black locks, molded her hands into his neck and shoulders, tasted his masculine goodness.

She'd practically thrown herself at him!

He'd turned her down.

Heat filled her cheeks. Had he come to gloat? Fine. Let him gloat. Perhaps he even deserved gloating rights. The man kissed like a dream.

She finished the call, hung up the phone, then met Sloan's gaze. "Can I help you?"

He didn't speak, just nodded, shut the door behind him, clicked the lock and crossed over to her desk. "Tell me I'm an idiot for leaving you last night."

That was an easy request to comply with. "You're an idiot for leaving me last night."

He laughed, took her hands and pulled her to her feet. "You enjoyed that too much."

"You are an idiot for leaving me last night," she repeated, enjoying saying the words again as she stared up into his eyes. Her heart raced and her head spun a little at his unexpected entrance into her office, at his unexpected words.

"I want to kiss you, Cara. Right now. Despite the fact that it's first thing in the morning and we've an office full of patients to see. I want to kiss you, because I didn't sleep for lying in bed, wishing I was kissing you."

Elation spread through her and she smiled up at him. "You are an idiot for leaving me last night," she said for a third time.

He laughed again and took her into his arms. She thought he would take her mouth, but he didn't. He just held her in his arms and brushed his lips across the top of her head.

"You're right," he whispered into her pulled-up hair. "I am an idiot for leaving you last night."

"Just so we're clear," she said matter-of-factly. "You are an idiot for leaving me last night."

He laughed yet again then became serious, leaned back to stare down at her. "I didn't want you to have regrets this morning and instead I'm the one with regrets."

She pulled away, walked across her office to collect her thoughts. "Actually, you were probably right to leave."

He frowned.

"But I can't say I was happy you did."

"How can I make it up to you?"

Giddiness percolated in her stomach, swelling to mammoth proportions in her chest and threatening to spill over as happy giggles. "We'll figure something out."

He nodded. "Soon."

"Sloan?"

"Hmm?"

"I don't want anyone to know."

"I wasn't planning on walking out of your office and making an announcement over the intercom system that we kissed."

She couldn't quite read his expression to know if he was annoyed or amused.

"I just thought we should be clear on that. I think this, whatever this is, should just be between you and me."

"As crystal."

"Are you upset?"

"No, I agree. This is something that should just be between you and me. No need to make people wonder what's going on when you'll be leaving in a couple of months."

Leaving in a couple of months. Two months and her time in Bloomberg would be over. She'd be able to leave and know she'd done as her father had wished. She'd leave and Sloan would stay. She'd never see him again. It was how life would be.

But she wouldn't think about that now.

"Then again, a lot can happen in two months," he surprised her by adding.

"True, but don't think I'll stay just because we get involved, Sloan. Living in Bloomberg would be a nightmare to me. Whatever happens between you and I has a two-month shelf life."

"Shelf life? You are so romantic," he accused, a grin spreading across his face.

"I'm being honest."

"Which I appreciate, but no worries. Two months works for me. I'm a confirmed bachelor, remember?"

She remembered, but someday some lucky Bloomberg woman would win his heart and they'd settle down into boring Bloomberg life and have a boring Bloomberg wedding and have boring Bloomberg babies. The thought made her ache a little inside, but she didn't fool herself that it could be any other way. Bloomberg life wasn't for her.

No matter what happened between her and Sloan, staying in Bloomberg was not an option.

Just look at what staying had done to her mother.

CHAPTER NINE

THE DAY DRAGGED. Each time Cara glanced at her watch mere minutes had passed when she felt as if hours should have come and gone. Surely Mother Nature had slowed down the passing of time?

Throughout the day, Cara saw routine medication refills, common colds, a few rashes and nothing out of the ordinary until Amie flagged her down.

"You might want to go into room two next. Abdominal pain. Nausea. Vomiting. Diarrhea. Says she feels as if she's dying. She's a walk-in and requested Sloan, but it's going to be a while before he's available to check her. He's in the middle of an ingrown toenail removal. She looks pretty miserable."

Cara's toes curled into the soles of her shoes. She'd done a few toenail removals during residency but none since. Thankfully, there weren't many opportunities for toenail removals in the emergency room. Just the thought of sticking a needle into someone's foot to do the nerve block gave her the heebie-jeebies. She'd gladly see the walk-in abdominal pain so long as he kept doing the toenail removals. "Gastroenteritis?"

"Maybe." But Amie didn't look convinced. Cara trusted the long-time nurse's instincts. Amie was good at what she did, which was why she'd been her father's nurse for so many years. "She's hurting in the left lower quadrant."

Left lower quadrant pain was oftentimes from constipation, but the woman had diarrhea. Perhaps a blockage or diverticulitis.

"Hmm. Possibly not just gastroenteritis, then, although it's still something to be ruled out," Cara mused, heading toward the room. "I'll check her now."

The young woman in her early twenties practically writhed on the examination table. Just looking at her made Cara's insides cramp in sympathy.

"I was hoping to see Dr. Trenton," the woman said immediately when she saw Cara.

Every single female from five to ninety hoped to see Dr. Trenton, Cara included.

"He's in with another patient at the moment. The nurse felt you should be seen as quickly as possible, rather than waiting, as he'll be in that room for a while."

The woman grimaced and nodded. "She's right. I'm pretty sure my insides are ripping apart. You'll do for now."

Cara didn't know whether to say thanks or not. The poor woman did look as if she felt as if her insides were being shredded. "When did your symptoms start?"

"This morning." The woman's arms crossed over her belly and she pulled inward. "I woke up in pain and the hurt just keeps getting worse."

"Have you taken anything?"

"Everything I could find." The woman mentioned several over-the-counter pain relievers and antacids. "Nothing helps."

Cara ran through a myriad of questions while looking over the girl's history. She hadn't had any surgeries so anything was a possibility.

Cara did a quick ENT and neck examination, then listened to her heart and lung sounds. All normal.

"Lie back on the table."

Amongst a lot of grunting and groaning, the woman lay back on the examination table. Her hands immediately covered her stomach. Eyes wide, she pleaded, "Be easy."

"I will be as easy as possible," Cara promised. "But I need to make sure I do a good assessment so we can figure out what's causing your symptoms. While I'm checking you, tell me what you've eaten the past twenty-four hours."

The only significant food intake was popcorn.

Cara finished examining the woman's abdomen, noting the extreme tenderness over her descending colon. "I think you have something called diverticulitis, which is an inflammation caused by bits of food that get trapped in pockets in the colon. Certain foods like seeds and popcorn kernels can get trapped. As the body tries to break them down, it causes cramping and a lot of the symptoms you're having."

Cara sat down at the small desk area and pulled out a form from the top desk drawer. "I'm going to send you over to the hospital to be admitted and to get some imaging of your abdomen and pelvis. I know your chart says no known drug allergies, but I like to confirm that. Are you allergic to anything, specifically any contrast dyes?"

The woman shook her head. "I don't have any allergies."

"Knock-knock," Sloan called through the closed examination room door, while actually knocking his knuckles against the door, as well.

"Come in," both Cara and the patient called.

"Hey, Stacey," he greeted the woman while he washed his hands. "What's going on?"

While he examined her, she ran through everything she'd told Cara, adding a few details about how much she hurt and how much she preferred seeing him to the new lady doctor. "I just prefer a man to check me. No offense meant," the girl added, with a quick look toward Cara.

"None taken," Cara assured her, signing her name to the hospital admission form she'd completed while Sloan was reexamining the woman.

"You getting a CT?"

Cara nodded. "I'm doing a direct admission with an urgent with-and-without-contrast CT order."

"Perfect." He turned back to the patient. "Looks like the new lady doctor has you on the right track. Do what she tells you to do and one of us will be by the hospital later today to check on you."

"I hope it's you." The woman nodded at him as if he hung the moon and dotted the sky with stars, as well.

Puh-leeze. Cara wanted to stick her finger in her mouth to make a gagging sound. Then again, she had kissed him and perhaps he had hung the moon and dotted the sky with stars. He'd been that good. But Stacey didn't know that.

Did she?

A streak of green a mile wide flashed hotly through Cara. A streak of green she'd never felt before. A streak of green she didn't like. She wasn't the jealous type. Sure, she and Sloan had kissed, but that didn't mean she had any right to feel possessive about him. To wonder about his relationships with other women. Now she wished she'd paid more attention when her father had been going on about all the women chasing after Sloan.

No, it didn't matter who was chasing him. They had no future together. Just a small wrinkle in time together.

"I'll get Amie to give you something for pain so long as you have someone to assist you next door," Cara offered, thinking that having Sloan in the room seemed to be working fairly well to distract the patient from her pain and distract *her* from everything but him, as well.

"My sister is in the waiting room. She can help me."

"Great," Cara said, determined to get back to professional because she didn't like the green monster inside her. "Amie will be in soon with something to ease your discomfort. I'm going to call the medical floor and let them know you are on your way over."

Cara paused outside Sloan's open office door. He sat at his desk, skimming over a paper, and then signed his name at the bottom.

Lord, he was a beautiful man. No wonder female patients preferred him and threw themselves at his feet. She couldn't blame them. Not that she planned to throw herself at his feet ever, but just looking at him could definitely make a person feel better.

Could justify a woman feeling possessive about him, could justify a woman feeling a little green that other women might have experienced those spectacular kisses.

She'd kissed him less than twenty-four hours before. And thrown herself at his feet. At all of him.

Heat flooded her body. How embarrassing. She'd never done anything of the sort before, but, at the time, having Sloan go home with her had seemed imperative.

Because she hadn't wanted to be alone because the teen's death had shaken her? Or because she'd wanted to be with Sloan?

If she was honest, she'd have to admit the truth had been a combination of both.

Sloan glanced up from his desk, catching her watching him. Good grief. He was probably going to start lumping her in the same category as all the other Sloan-starved women in Bloomberg. No wonder. She *was* Sloan-starved. Pathetic.

"What did Stacey's CT show?"

"Definitely diverticulitis, with a possible perforated colon."

"Ouch." He set his ink pen down on the desk and motioned for her to come into his office. "She really was in pain."

Cara's heartbeat took on a wild jungle tempo. Any moment she expected her mouth to open and a Tarzan call to echo around the building. That's how wild her heart beat in her chest. The image of Sloan in a leopard-skin loincloth popped into her head. She imagined the planes of the body she'd been pressed up against at the ball field. Strong, hard, chiseled. Would he have chest hair or have a smooth chest? In her vision, she imagined he'd have at least a smattering of chest hair that tapered down a southward path.

"I've requested a surgical consult," she said to ground herself in reality, walking into the room and sitting down in a chair across from him. She crossed her legs then immediately uncrossed them and tucked her hands under her thighs to keep from fidgeting. "Anything else you want ordered since she is technically your patient?"

He studied her for a few moments then offered, "I can take over her admission, if you prefer."

Flustered that her awkwardness was coming across

all wrong, Cara shook her head. "No. I've got her taken care of."

"Are you okay?"

She didn't need to ask why he'd think she might not be. She was acting like a nervous schoolgirl. What was wrong with her? This so wasn't her. "I'm fine. It's just been a long day."

"Can I buy you dinner to make up for it?"

"For my having a long day?"

"Just imagine how long my day would have been if you'd not been here."

"True, but you don't owe me anything, Sloan. I'm doing this for my father. No other reason."

"I know that. But I do appreciate you being here. I know Bloomberg is not where you want to be."

She shook her head. "You're right. It's not."

But was there anywhere she'd rather be at this moment than with him? No. No. No. She wasn't going to think that way.

He leaned back in his chair. "Tell me, Cara, what is it about Bloomberg that you dislike so much?"

"Everything," she answered immediately.

"I don't believe you."

She arched her brow at him.

"Come on, there must be something about the place you like."

"I like being so close to the gulf."

He looked surprised. "Have you been to the beach since coming home?"

"Every chance I get. I've driven down every weekend I've not been on call."

"Let's go." He shocked her by saying it.

What? "We can't go to the beach."

"Why not?"

"Well, for starters, we've admitted Stacey Jones and already have two patients on the medical floor. Plus, I'm on call tonight."

"That's right." He shrugged, then grinned. "We'll go this weekend."

She opened her mouth to say no. She didn't need to go to the gulf with him.

"Casey is on call this weekend," he reminded her before she got a word out. "There's no reason we couldn't drive down on Friday night after we finish here. We could come back on Sunday afternoon."

"Spend the entire weekend with you?"

He searched her face, no doubt trying to read her thoughts. "Yes. Spend the weekend at the beach with me, Cara."

She knew what he was saying, what would happen if they went away together. There could be no regrets of having been caught up in the moment. If she said yes, it was because she wanted him. Wanted them.

She didn't want them, but she couldn't deny that she wanted him. Which made no sense. She didn't have flings. But if she agreed to go with him, wasn't that exactly what she'd be agreeing to? They had no future, no possibility of a future. A fling was all there was to be had between them.

She hesitated. "I thought we agreed this morning that we didn't want anyone to know. We can't both disappear for the weekend. Everyone will know we're together."

"You'll be leaving before long and you'll never have to see these people again. What anyone in Bloomberg thinks won't matter in the slightest."

"Good point, but what about you? You plan to stay in Bloomberg forever. Surely you don't want a fling with me ruining your reputation?"

"I wouldn't call our going to the beach together a 'fling'."

She knew what their going away together for a weekend would entail. How they labeled the weekend didn't change what would happen. "How would you describe our going to the beach together?"

Sloan thought a minute, then met her gaze and took her breath away with the intensity in his coppery eyes. "A fantasy come true."

She bit into her lower lip, barely registering the metallic twang that filled her mouth. "You make it impossible to say no."

He grinned. "Good, because you saying no isn't the idea. I want you to say yes."

A slow smile spread across her face. "I hope I don't live to regret this but okay, Sloan. I will go to the beach with you this weekend."

Sloan couldn't believe she'd said yes so quickly. He felt like jumping into the air and pumping his fist. Instead, he just smiled. "You know what will happen if we go away together?"

"We'll get sunburned?" she asked, blinking innocently.

"We may not even see the sun."

"I know," she admitted on a sigh, looking a little pensive. "It's inevitable. It has been from the morning I woke up kissing you."

"You've thought about that morning?" He wished they weren't at the office, weren't where anyone could come interrupt them. Okay, Amie was the only one who hadn't gone home for the day. No doubt she would approve. She'd said more than one thing to that effect since Cara had started at the clinic. Then again, Amie and Preston had been close. She probably knew what Preston wanted, what he'd asked of Sloan.

Cara's thoughts obviously going where his had, she glanced over her shoulder down the empty office hallway. "I've got to go to the hospital to check on Stacey."

Sloan laughed. "Chicken."

"A wise girl knows when to speak and when to hold her tongue."

"Silence can be an answer in and of itself."

"Silence is what I expect from you regarding this weekend. Like I said, regardless of whether or not I'm leaving in two months, I don't want my private business discussed all over town. If for no other reason than out of respect for my father."

"I respect that."

"I'm sure you do," she said, stared at him a moment with something akin to dislike, then took off to disappear down the hallway, turning at the last moment to meet his gaze. "I'm off to pack my bikini. Have a good evening."

Imagining her in a bikini, Sloan groaned.

Lust was a crazy thing. No doubt Cara wasn't the first woman to fall into lust with the wrong man. Not that Sloan was a bad man. He wasn't. She wasn't so obstinate that she couldn't see all his good qualities and what a blessing he was to Bloomberg. On that matter, she understood her father. But she wasn't into affairs and that was all she and Sloan could ever have.

Whether she was into affairs or not, she'd essentially agreed to have one. With Sloan. Crazy.

Would they only have this weekend or did he intend them to continue until she left Bloomberg?

To continue beyond this weekend would just be asking for trouble, would be asking for feelings to develop between them that she didn't need.

She'd go this weekend, get her fill of Sloan and then they'd go back to being coworkers, only the sexual tension between them would be abated because they wouldn't be wondering about each other. A perfect plan. Or so she kept telling herself.

Friday evening seemed to take forever to come and yet it got there before Cara was ready. She'd spent longer in the bathroom the night before than she had in years. She'd shaved, waxed, plucked, buffed, lotioned, perfumed and conditioned herself until she knew she'd done all she could to look good in Sloan's eyes.

She wanted to look good in his eyes.

Crazy, because she knew he wanted her. He'd told her as much and she saw it in how he looked at her. Each day the tension between them had continued to build, to the point that just seeing him or hearing his voice revved her engines.

A man as beautiful as Sloan had probably had a lot of women, but she refused to think about that, about her lack of experience. All that mattered was that this weekend the two of them would assuage the heat that burned between them, and then they'd be done.

"Hi," she said, trying not to sound nervous when she let him into her father's house.

"You ready?"

"As ready as I'm ever going to be."

He laughed. "That sounds more as if you're going for a colonoscopy than away to the beach for the weekend."

"Sorry. I'm a little nervous."

"That's okay, Cara." He moved close to her, cupped her face. "I understand. I couldn't sleep last night for thinking about us."

She took a deep breath and knew she needed to clarify one more time the boundaries of their weekend. "There is no us. What happens between us physically this weekend is all that there can ever be."

"You can deny it all you want, but we both know there is an us."

Cara's stomach churned. "Not beyond this weekend, there's not."

"Do you really believe that?"

"For us to go beyond this weekend would be foolish. There's absolutely no chance of anything further happening between us. I won't risk it."

"Risk it?"

"Being entangled in a relationship in Bloomberg."

"You don't think this weekend will make you feel entangled in a relationship with me?"

"I won't let it," she admitted. "I won't stay in Bloomberg and one, or possibly both, of us will end up hurt if we pretend otherwise."

His grip on her face tightened just the slightest, then he stroked his fingers down the side of her cheek. "You're right. Only this weekend it is, then."

Relief flooded her that he'd agreed. Some other twinge of something also flooded her but she wasn't sure what that emotion was so she smiled and focused on the man in front of her. "Come on. The beach is calling my name."

While she locked up the house, he grabbed her suitcase and stowed it in the back of his Jeep.

"Are we staying in a hotel?"

He shook his head. "I've rented a one-bedroom house on Santa Rosa Island."

A house. More privacy. Good.

"I love Santa Rosa." She fastened her hair back so the

wind wouldn't whip it around so crazily when they took off. "My parents used to go there when I was a baby."

It was the one place where her mother had been happy. She'd looked so carefree and content in the photos taken there. Just as her father had.

"I know. I've seen photos."

Pausing with her hands still in her hair, her brows shot up. "How have you seen photos of that?"

There weren't any large framed shots of their family outings on her father's office wall or even anywhere in the house. Just some four-by-six shots taken on her mother's camera that were stuck into an old album and some photos of her mother laughing on the beach that he'd kept in his bedroom.

Sloan shrugged and started the ignition. "Your father showed me your photos one night when we were at his place. Your mother was a beautiful woman. You look a lot like her."

Elation filled her at his statement that she looked like her mother. But shock also hit her.

"Dad pulled out old photo albums?" That so didn't sound like Dr. Preston Conner. He hadn't been a man given to sentimental gestures.

"He was very proud of you."

She laughed a little nervously, not sure what she thought of her father and Sloan having pored over old family albums. What else had her father shared with Sloan? A twinge of jealousy hit her that her father had sat and looked at the old albums with Sloan, something she couldn't recall him ever having done with her. Then again, Sloan had been like a son to him and he'd always wanted a son. Doubt hit her.

All the old feelings about her father and Sloan were still there, but new feelings were there, too. Feelings that kept her from demanding he take her home. Feelings that had her simply saying, "I'm sorry you had to suffer through baby photos of me."

"I'm not. I enjoyed them." He actually sounded as if he really had.

"Why?"

"Why wouldn't I? I cared deeply for Preston and he cared deeply for you."

She sank her teeth into her lower lip, wincing when she caught an already sore spot.

They rode in silence until they were a few miles outside Bloomberg.

"How did you end up in Bloomberg?" she asked, curious as to how he'd come to such a tiny town to practice. He was good enough to work anywhere he wanted. Why Bloomberg?

"I was working in Columbia, Ohio, and met Preston at a medical conference in Nashville. He convinced me that I'd enjoy small-town practice a lot more than living in the city. It didn't take much. I'd always planned to move to a small town to practice someday."

"And settle down?"

"I do want to marry and have kids but, obviously, I'm not in a rush."

She nodded. Women would line up to audition for the role.

"What about you?" he asked, glancing toward her. "What's next on your life agenda after your Bloomberg stint?"

She shrugged. "Back to New York."

"Back to pick up where you left off?"

"I let John…" Her voice trailed off.

"That's your ex?"

She nodded. "Sorry. Anyway, I let him have the lease

on my apartment. I quit my job when I came here. I love the city, so I'll go back there, but I'll probably work at a different facility."

"To avoid seeing your ex?"

"Not really. We're still friends and have talked a few times since I've been here."

That seemed to shock him and he asked, "Do you think you'll get back together when you return to New York?"

She shook her head. Of that she was positive. Whatever had been between John and herself wasn't what she wanted for the rest of her life. Yes, they'd had fun together on their adventures and both had felt passionate about their trips. Too bad they'd not felt as passionately about each other. Too bad neither of them had realized that.

"I may take a few months off before going back to work, maybe travel a bit, do some mission work, while I figure out what I want to do the rest of my life." She was thinking out loud, testing the idea as she said it.

"Maybe you could do a travel medicine stint. Sign on for a year or something," he suggested.

"Maybe." Why did his offering suggestions on places for her to go sting? It wasn't as if either of them expected her to stay in Bloomberg so to be hurt was just ridiculous.

He pulled onto the main highway and the increased speed made further chitchat seem silly as they'd practically have to yell at each other to be heard over the wind noise.

Cara flipped the radio station on then, curious about what type of music he chose to listen to, she hit the CD button.

"Johnny Cash? Really?" she called toward him, her

hair whipping about her face despite her earlier efforts to contain it.

He glanced her way then grinned.

No wonder her father had been so crazy about Sloan. Johnny Cash had been her father's all-time favorite. Medicine, Bloomberg and Johnny. Sloan really was her dad's mini-me.

Which was yet another reason why she shouldn't be with him this weekend, but she wasn't going to worry about that. Instead, she planned to not worry about anything beyond the weekend. Time enough for that later.

Sloan paid the toll going onto the Santa Rosa Island Bridge and stole a peek at Cara. She had been antsy the entire drive. They'd started the trip talking, but once on the highway they had settled into singing along with the radio. Now she refused to even look his way.

She was such a contradiction. Strong, fiercely independent, yet vulnerable and unsure of herself. She was nervous about this weekend.

So was he.

She'd lived with a man in New York, so he didn't kid himself that she was inexperienced. But, other than John, he'd never heard her father mention other boyfriends or men in her life. Sure, he'd seen photographic evidence of high-school dance dates and the like, but no guy had ever managed to be in more than one photo. Interesting, that.

Had she never let herself get close enough to anyone in Bloomberg because she hadn't wanted to risk falling for someone there?

Once onto the island, Sloan turned left at the main intersection and headed east past hotels and a few restaurants and shops. Soon they were in a more residential section of the island. He made a right turn and within minutes he was pulling the car up to the beachfront bungalow-style house he'd rented.

"This looks nice," Cara said, hopping out of the Jeep and reaching for her bag out of the backseat.

"I hope the inside looks as great as it did online." He grabbed his bag and tried to take hers from her, but she refused to let him. He unlocked the door with the pass code the rental agency had given him.

"You haven't been here before?" Cara asked once they were inside. The decor was very typical beach house. Lots of blues, whites, shells, sailboats and a framed print of a lighthouse that dominated the airy room.

"No." He walked into the bedroom, set his suitcase down, then turned back to her. "I have visited the beach with a few friends who came down from Ohio to visit and have made a few day trips, but that's the extent of my beach trips."

She put her suitcase on the bed and began unpacking. "Some friends had beach houses in Atlantic City that we'd stay in from time to time, but the beaches up north just aren't the same as the white beaches here."

She continued to unpack and talk, almost as if she was afraid for there to be a second's silence between them.

"Come on," he said, when she had almost finished unpacking her bag and was still prattling on about New Jersey beaches. "Let's go for a walk."

"But I thought…" Her gaze went to the bed, then jerked back to him. Tension poured off her body. The same tension that had continued to increase on their drive.

"That I brought you up here to immediately ravage

you and that I didn't plan to let you have a moment's peace?"

Her face flushed.

He walked over, took her hands. "We have all weekend, Cara. Let's walk, then we can grab something to eat. I paid the rental agency extra to stock a few items in the fridge for breakfast and snacks, but I've been looking forward to some fresh seafood all day."

He'd been looking forward to kissing her, too, but this weekend wasn't just about sex for him. He wanted to spend time with Cara, to get to know her away from Bloomberg. He wanted her relaxed.

She smiled. "Sounds good. I love the beach."

He took her hand and they took off toward the water, being careful not to disturb the dune as they crossed over to the beach.

Cara let go of his hand and, laughing and kicking off her sandals, raced to the water, pausing as waves lapped at her bare feet.

Turning, she smiled at him. "Sugar-sand beaches, gorgeous blue water, very few people, and just smell the breeze." She inhaled deeply. "Don't you just love Santa Rosa?"

"I do now."

She laughed and ran her hands through the water, sending a spray his way. "Come on and get wet. Unless you're chicken."

He laughed. There went that competitive spirit.

He got into the water then surprised her by sending a large splash her way. She didn't squeal or squirm away, just went on the attack and soaked him.

Laughing, they splashed each other, then he caught her by the waist and spun her around. A wave shifted the sand beneath his feet, sucking it outward and he lost his footing.

"Oh!" she yelped, as they plopped down into the water.

"Come on." He grabbed her hand and helped her onto her feet. "Let's get that walk in before the next wave pummels us."

She glanced down at her soaked clothes. "Not like it would matter much at this point."

Her clothes were plastered to her body, outlining her lean shape. Sloan gulped and tried to sound normal. "Do you want to go inside and change into dry clothes?"

Oblivious that his mind had gone from playful to wanting to throw her over his shoulder and carry her to their bedroom and do exactly as she'd been expecting on their arrival, she shook her head. "Nope. We're supposed to be wet. We're at the beach."

Struggling to get his body under control, because his clothes were wet, too, Sloan watched her pluck the material away from her skin and fan it outward. He wasn't sure how much that was going to help dry the material, but it wasn't doing a thing for his imagination. Maybe she'd been right and they should have just gotten sex over with to break the tension between them.

At the moment the anticipation of peeling her clothes off her was about to kill him. But he'd always been a patient man, and now wasn't the time to waver from that lifelong course.

This weekend was monumental and Sloan knew it. What happened between them would be a turning point in their relationship. Either in a good way or a bad way.

It was up to him to steer them in a good direction.

Hand in hand, they walked, stopping to pick up a shell here and there. By the time they'd walked, turned and got back to the house he'd rented, Sloan was a mess, but Cara was a relaxed beach bum. She hummed as he sprayed the sand off her feet with a water hose. Water trickled over her rosy-pink toenails. He brushed off a stubborn bit of sand and couldn't resist running his fingertip up the side of her foot.

"Hey, no fair," she protested, wiggling out of his grasp.

"Ticklish?"

"Obviously." She moved away from the water spicket. "I'm going to change while you wash the sand off, then let's go find some of that fresh seafood you were talking about. I'm starved."

Sloan was, too, but crab legs weren't what were foremost in his mind.

"So you never knew your parents?" Cara asked, cracking open another crab leg and sucking out the delicious meat inside.

His gaze zeroed in on her mouth, Sloan shook his head.

Cara bit back a smile at his expression. Okay, so perhaps it was wrong of her, but since she'd relaxed, she'd been enjoying herself. A great deal. Sex appeal and her father aside, Sloan really was a great guy.

Okay, so the sex appeal definitely played into her current merriment. Sloan wanted her. And she was enjoying every second of their foreplay.

There could be no more accurate name for what passed between them. Sure, some might call it dinner and conversation, but she knew what it really was.

Every word, every expression, every touch, whether intentional or accidental, were all preludes to what the night would hold.

She'd never considered herself a tease or a seductress but, with Sloan watching her, she felt like a sultry combination of both. Because every move she made turned him on and she liked it. A lot.

Just as she liked him. A lot.

Beneath the table, she slid one foot out of her sandal and slid her toes along the hairy plane of his shin. "There wasn't anyone else who could take you in?"

Eyebrow lifting at her under-the-table play, he shook his head. "I have a few aunts and uncles, but they had their hands full with their own kids. I went into the foster-care system at six and stayed there until I graduated high school. It wasn't so bad. My last foster family was good to me, encouraged me to apply for scholarships and go to college. I still talk to them every so often, but haven't seen them in years."

"I can't imagine." She really couldn't. Her admiration for him, for what he'd accomplished in life, rose even higher, as did the foot that toyed along his leg. She stretched, grazing her toes behind to his calf.

He took a long haul of his drink. "This is perhaps the strangest conversation I've ever had."

"Why's that?" she asked, truly curious and liking the hard calf muscles her toes toyed with.

He leaned toward her, his eyes locked with hers. "Because this topic isn't one I like talking about. It's usually a total turn-off."

"But?"

He took her hand into his. "I'm not turned off."

Excitement fluttered through her body. "You find the conversation stimulating?"

"Something like that." He gestured to her plate. "You about done?"

She didn't even glance down, just held his gaze. "Not nearly."

His lips twitched. "Want dessert?"

"Something like that." She tossed his words back at him but made no move to eat another bite. She didn't want food and they both knew it.

He glanced at the ticket, pulled out his wallet and threw down a few twenties. "Let's go."

Not hesitating, she slipped her sandal back on and took his hand.

He helped her into the Jeep, then drove the few miles down the road to their house. The moment he parked the car under the covered porch Cara hopped out of the vehicle and took off up the stairs. Why, she couldn't exactly say, just that she didn't want to linger in the car with him. When he made it to the top of the stairs he found her leaning over the balcony, staring out at the moonlit waves.

"It's so beautiful and peaceful here. It's like all the cares of the world just vanish. Like nothing else matters or exists."

"It doesn't," he agreed, causing her to turn to look at him.

The breeze caught at his hair, toying with the dark tufts. His eyes were dark molten copper pools that beckoned her to take a plunge.

She planned to. She planned to dive in and not look back.

"I want you," she told him with all honesty.

"The feeling is mutual," he assured her, unlocking the house door, pushing it open, then moving to stand beside her, his hands at her waist. "So very mutual."

She didn't wait for him to kiss her. Instead, she took what she wanted. Him. She couldn't say she exactly launched herself at him but she probably couldn't deny it if accused, either.

Either way, within seconds her body was wrapped around his, melting against him, kissing him as she clung to him. The sound of the waves behind them played the perfect melody. His hands moved over her body, cupped her bottom, molding her tighter against his hard frame.

Her inner thighs squeezed, hugging his hips, eliciting a husky growl from deep within his throat.

"I want you here."

Did he think she was going to argue with him? She wasn't. She was burning up for him, yearning to feel him inside her.

"But I want to see you. All of you."

She'd just as soon he didn't, but was too far gone to argue. Especially when him seeing her meant she'd get to see him, too.

He carried her inside the house and into the bedroom. She slid down him, went to reach for his shirt, but he moved away, opened the sliding glass door that opened onto the balcony. Sounds of the waves crashing against the beach filled the room, but he left the curtains drawn, blocking the view and protecting their privacy should anyone be walking along the beach.

"Nice," she said as he flicked on a bedside lamp.

"Very," he agreed, pulling his T-shirt over his head.

"Oh, my," she breathed. Sure, she'd known he was buff beneath his clothes, but the man was gorgeous. How many hours did he spend working out a week, anyway? She knew he ran most mornings before the crack of dawn, played and coached sports, but he got in some gym time at some point, too.

"Your turn."

Cara gave a slightly nervous laugh then complied, lifting her shirt over her head to reveal her silky bra. His intake of breath was all she needed to boost her confidence another notch, and without questioning herself she hooked her fingers into her shorts and slid them down her hips. She stood before him in her cream-colored silk bra and panties and let him look.

She wasn't in as good a shape as she'd been a few years back and should have felt self-conscious, but under his gaze she just felt beautiful. How could she not when his eyes ate her up and his voice broke when he said her name?

"Your turn," she said, using his words because she wanted to look at him, too. She wanted to see him, to touch him, to caress and taste him.

He outdid her, of course, removing both his shorts and his boxers together. Naked, he stood before her.

Cara swallowed. He'd been right. Whatever happened between them would be huge.

But she didn't have time to think anything else because he closed the distance between them and began touching and kissing her. All rational thought disappeared and wouldn't be found until long after the sun came up.

Cara's soft moans and undulations against him were driving Sloan wild. He'd been fighting the urge to strip her panties off her and take what he wanted for what had seemed like eons but which had probably only been minutes.

He made haste with her bra, tossed back the bedspread and pushed her down onto their bed. She lay there looking up at him with eager eyes and he almost lost it.

But he got a grip on himself and slowed himself down. He wanted this to be good for her. He wanted her as starved for him as he was for her. He moved atop her and kissed her. He kissed her mouth, her throat and her breasts.

"Sloan," she cried against the top of his head, clasping her fingers into his hair. He smiled. She was getting close. So very close.

He teased her with his tongue, over and over, back and forth, until she cried out his name again. Then he moved lower and pulled off her panties. Within seconds she was whimpering, moving against him, tugging him toward her.

"Please. I need you."

Sloan had enough sense to get out a condom he'd put in the end table drawer earlier and slipped it on.

"Hurry," she pleaded, pulling him to her. "Sloan. Please."

He moved between her legs, kept himself raised off her and positioned himself at her entrance. Rather than push inside, he met her gaze and waited, watching her face, looking into her passion-filled eyes and knowing he'd done that. He'd put that expression on her face.

Never had she looked more beautiful to him.

Her fingers found his shoulders and dug in. Her pelvis lifted and he slid inside and knew what he'd been denying to himself for months.

His gaze met hers and he wondered if she could see the depth of his emotions. Either way, it didn't matter because he couldn't hide what suddenly felt so obvious.

"I've been waiting for this moment for a lifetime."

CHAPTER TEN

CARA COULDN'T GET enough of Sloan. Not at the beach. Not after they returned to Bloomberg. So what if Gladys Jones had baked several batches of brownies that had been delivered with questions about Sloan's Jeep spending the night at her place?

So what if everyone at the clinic looked at them with knowing smiles?

They hadn't told a soul, but so what if they all knew, anyway?

Cara didn't care. She'd thought she would, but the reality of being with Sloan was so much more than she could have ever imagined.

For the past two months she'd walked around in a daze. A happy, euphoric daze of working side by side with Sloan and burning up the nights with him.

Like tonight, for instance. She stretched out in his bed, happy, content, her body achy, but in an, oh, so good way.

They usually went to her house, but tonight they'd called by his place to pick up a change of clothes for the morning and they'd ended up in his bed.

They had not talked about what would happen in two days when her time in Bloomberg was up.

Honestly, she wasn't sure herself what was going to

happen. John had called her, told her he missed her and that she was welcome to move back into their apartment.

That one had been easy.

Several of her friends who worked at the hospital had called, asked her about returning to her old job. That had been more difficult.

She'd liked her life before her return to Bloomberg, had liked her job and her coworkers, but the idea of going back didn't appeal as much as it should.

But she would go back.

Not to John.

Or even to her previous job most likely. She'd find a new challenge, something where she gave more back within the community she chose to live in, and she'd make a new life for herself. A better one than she'd had before.

A better one than she had now. Which currently seemed pretty impossible.

If only Sloan wasn't meant to stay in Bloomberg.

"What are you thinking about?"

She rolled over, tucking the sheet under her arm, and smiled at him. "Nothing."

"Your expression went from happy to sour."

Should she tell him?

"You were thinking about New York?"

Could he read her mind?

She shrugged. "I guess that's normal as my time here is almost up."

"Just because your six months is up it doesn't mean you have to leave immediately, Cara. Unless you've lined up something you haven't mentioned, there isn't a reason to rush back to your old life."

"I haven't lined up another job yet."

"Then what would staying a few more weeks hurt?

You can take your time and figure out what it is you want from life."

What indeed?

Part of her feared she'd never be ready to leave so long as Sloan was there, but eventually this heat between them would burn out and the glittery shine would fade and then leaving would be easy, right? She really didn't have to rush away.

"I want you to stay, Cara." He traced his fingers over her bare arm, causing her flesh to goose-bump. "Stay with me."

She closed her eyes and tried to picture being back in New York, being away from Sloan. All she saw was the misery and loneliness of missing him.

All she saw if she stayed was ending up like her mother. Her mother had wanted more for her than Bloomberg. Cara wanted more than Bloomberg.

Not answering him, she ran her fingers along the muscles in his shoulders, liking the way his flesh responded similarly to how hers had.

Searching her eyes so intently her breath caught, he took her hand in his. "In case you haven't noticed, I'm in love with you, Cara. Tell me you'll stay with me."

Forever. The word wasn't said, but Cara heard it all the same. The air between them tensed and she felt as if they were talking about a lot more than just a few weeks. An invisible fist tightened around her throat and she struggled to breathe as claustrophobia set in.

Sloan had just said he was in love with her. Could it be true? Did she want it to be true?

She must because her heart was making ecstatic leaps in her chest. But fear gripped her, too. Fear that if she said the wrong thing, she'd end up a shriveled ghost of a woman, the way her mother had. Some said pancreatic cancer had killed her mother, but Cara had always believed she'd died of a broken heart.

"I will leave Bloomberg, Sloan. Maybe not when I originally planned, but I will leave this place. To stay would suffocate me."

He nodded as if he understood, but she was pretty sure he didn't. She leaned forward to kiss him, to re-assure him that she didn't plan to leave any time soon, but to her surprise he got out of bed.

"I'm going to grab a shower," he said, without turn-ing around.

Cara watched him walk into the bathroom and re-played their conversation. He'd told her he loved her and she'd focused on the leaving part. No wonder he was upset.

But did he really think she was just going to let him walk away from her in mid-conversation like that? To tell her he loved her and then take a shower alone? Wrong.

Knowing where her going into the bathroom with him was likely to lead, she opened his nightstand drawer to get a condom out of the box she knew he kept there.

She pulled the condom out and was shutting the drawer when an envelope caught her eye.

An envelope very similar to one she had. Same hand-writing. Different name.

She shouldn't touch it. Had no right to touch. But her fingers couldn't not touch it.

She traced Sloan's name, fighting an onslaught of conflicting emotions.

Her father had written his name. Just as he'd writ-ten the letter inside.

She pulled her hand away and closed the drawer. She had no right to read Sloan's letter. No matter how curious she was about what her father had told him. She had no right.

So why wasn't she on her way to join him in the shower, as she'd intended? Why was she reopening a drawer she had no right to open? Opening an envelope she had no right to look inside?

God, that woman frustrated him to no end. How could she be so blind to what they shared? To how special and amazing what was happening between them was?

She was so intent on making sure she left Bloomberg that she'd blinded herself to the truth. Or maybe he was the one blinded?

Blinded with love.

He'd known better. Known that an emotional entanglement with Cara was a bad idea, but he'd been emotionally entangled with her long before he'd met her in person.

He'd fallen in love with her through her father. He'd gotten to know her through Preston's eyes and heart and he'd fallen hard. No wonder every woman he'd tried to date had fallen so short when he'd compared them to Cara. Because she'd already had him.

The stubborn woman would leave him just to leave Bloomberg, even if it wasn't what she wanted. Not that she knew what she wanted. She didn't. Not other than him. He wasn't so blind that he didn't know exactly how much she wanted him. She enjoyed their time together as much as he did. She craved their time together as much as he did. Not just for sex, but for their runs, their trips to the beach, when she'd taken on helping him coach his T-ball team, when they rounded together at the hospital, consulted each other regarding patients. They were perfect together. Only they weren't together.

Because if he asked her if they were a couple, she'd say no, they weren't. In her eyes they were having a short-term fling.

He tossed his head back, letting the hot water run over his hair, down his shoulders.

He should be in his bed, reminding her of all the reasons why she shouldn't leave Bloomberg, the number-one reason being him.

When he kissed her, she didn't talk about leaving. When he kissed her, she begged for more, gave more, gave everything.

He rinsed, towel-dried himself, then wrapped the towel around his waist. She may plan to leave, but she wasn't gone yet and he planned to show her all the reasons why she should stay.

"Look, Cara, I'm sorry if you feel like I'm pushing you to stay, but the reality is I don't want you to leave and I'm not going to pretend otherwise."

Her back was to him and he couldn't see what she was doing. If he'd thought about it, he'd have realized something was up, but he was already upset over the prospect of her leaving.

"I am never going to want you to leave, because I meant what I said. I'm in love with you and I think you love me, too."

That's when she turned and he saw what she held.

His gaze lifted to hers, saw her tears, and a sinking feeling took hold of his insides and plummeted.

"How could you?" she accused.

"How could I what?" Preston's letter didn't say anything that Sloan had done, just requested things Preston wanted him to do, such as convince Cara to stay.

"It must be great to have my father's blessing regarding all this." She stretched her hand out over their love-tangled sheets.

"He suggested I marry you, not take you to my bed."

"Guess that one stretched the limits of your friend-ship too far, eh?"

Sloan closed his eyes, took a deep breath and recalled exactly what Preston's letter had said. He'd read the thing so many times he could quote it word for word. "I wouldn't marry you or anyone just because Preston wanted me to."

"No, you didn't think you'd have to. You'd just make me want you so much that I couldn't bear the thought of leaving you."

"Do you, Cara? Do you want me that much?"

"No," she burst out immediately. "Whatever I felt, this killed it all." She waved the letter between them. "How dare he use you to coerce me to stay? How dare he?"

Sloan didn't answer. He didn't agree with Preston's methods, but he knew why. Preston had figured out that Sloan had feelings for Cara. No wonder. He'd prob-ably been as obvious as a brick through a windshield. How many times had he asked Preston about her, if he'd talked to her recently? How many nights had he and Preston sat around, talking about Cara? Too many.

Thank God he'd declined Preston's attempt to bring him to New York for that last conference he'd attended. No doubt he'd have played matchmaker right then and there, despite the fact Cara had been living with an-other man.

What a tangled mess they'd weaved.

Sloan,
    My last wish and desire is that my daughter move home to Bloomberg. It's where she belongs even if she doesn't realize it. It's where she's al-ways belonged. You probably think I'm crazy for

the wheels I've set into motion, but I know my daughter and I know you, son.

My death will have brought her home. Please see to it that she rediscovers Bloomberg and its people. Bloomberg is her heritage and a part of who she is, even if she doesn't want to admit it. If I'd ever had a son, I would have wanted him to have been like you.

Nothing would have made me happier than for you to have married my daughter and truly been my son. You're exactly the kind of man Cara needs in her life. Exactly the kind of man I want for her. Please take care of her.

My biggest regret is that in my grief over losing my wife and throwing myself into work to help me cope day by day, I failed Cara. In my death, I don't want to do the same.

You are a man of integrity. I know I can trust you to help her heal old wounds she doesn't even realize she has. Take care of my daughter, Sloan. If I ever meant anything to you, take care of my daughter and raise my grandchildren in Bloomberg.

Preston

Hands shaking, Cara dropped the letter that had scalded her insides. She shouldn't have read Sloan's letter. To have done so was wrong.

But for her father to have asked Sloan to take care of her, to marry her, was just as wrong.

More wrong.

Anger coursed through her. Anger at her father. Anger at Sloan. What kind of game was he playing with her? And why?

"Cara?" Sloan walked around to where she sat on the bed. A towel hugged his narrow hips. She wanted to scream that her body responded to his nearness, to his beautiful nakedness.

She didn't want to want him.

Not now.

Not when she suddenly questioned every kindness he'd ever shown her. Not when she suddenly questioned every look, every touch, every word.

"Why?"

Sloan stared down at where she sat, but he didn't answer her question.

She stood, wrapping the sheet around her as she did so. She stretched on her tiptoes, not wanting to be at any disadvantage to him. "Tell me why, damn it!"

"I can't explain his letter."

"I'm not talking about his letter. I'm asking why you did it."

"Did what?"

"Went along with his stupid request. How could you do that? Why would you do that?"

"I didn't."

"Yes, you did."

"No, Cara, I didn't."

"That—" she motioned to where the letter had landed on the floor beside them "—isn't what the past six months has been about?"

"No. Not really." He raked his fingers through his hair, the motion stretching his arm, flexing his chest muscles.

She closed her eyes, let her anger consume all other emotions. "You told me once there wasn't anything you wouldn't have done for my father."

His voice took on an angry quality of its own. "Don't say it, Cara, because you know it's not true."

"Do I?" She opened her eyes, glared at him. "Do I really know that you haven't just been buttering me up for the past six months so you could convince me to stay?"

"You told me earlier tonight you aren't staying so that would have been a pointless endeavor, now, wouldn't it?"

"And you told me you loved me," she accused, anger and hurt overwhelming her, making her legs wobble and her heart shatter. She hit his chest with her fist, the sheet still tightly gripped in her fingers. "How could you say something like that when you didn't mean it?"

"What do you care? It's not as if the words meant anything to you or as if you said the words back to me."

Had that stung? That she'd failed to return his words? With all the Bloomberg women falling at his feet, that she'd resisted his claim of love must have stung.

"Oh, you'd really have liked that, wouldn't you?" she blasted. "If I fell in love with you and then you could manipulate me into doing whatever you wanted?"

He took a deep breath, put his hands over her fist, and held it still against his chest. "I could see how you would equate love with manipulation, Cara, but what I told you had nothing to do with Preston's letter. I wanted you to stay for me."

Even in her anger, she couldn't deny her body's response to his touch, to his bare chest with the trail of hair that ran down his flat abs and disappeared beneath the towel. Good Lord, even the man's bare feet got to her. But for once her body's reaction to him just fueled her anger. Never had she felt so betrayed.

By her body. Her father. Sloan.

Sloan was with her because her father had asked him to be with her.

"You can stop pretending."

His grip remained tight on her hands. "What do you mean? Pretending?"

"You told me in the same breath as you said you loved me that you wanted me to stay," she reminded him. "I know you were just trying to convince me to stay so you could give my father what he wanted."

"I do want you to stay." His forehead creased. "Or I did."

Or he had. Implying he no longer did. Because she knew everything now?

"Fine. It doesn't matter, anyway, because I'm not staying." She jerked her hand free, dropped the sheet and picked her clothes up off the floor. "There's nothing in Bloomberg I want and nothing that could convince me to stay in this horrible town."

CHAPTER ELEVEN

A BLAST OF frigid air hit Cara in the face as she stepped outside her apartment building. She pulled her coat and scarf tighter around her body and reminded herself that she loved this city.

She did. She just...

Oh, no, she wasn't going there. Not this morning. Today was a new day and today she wasn't going to think about Bloomberg or Sloan or anything from the South. She wasn't.

Six weeks had gone by since she'd flown home to New York. Six weeks in which she'd cried her silly heart out to her ex and he'd offered to let her stay in his spare bedroom. She'd taken him up on the offer for a couple of nights, but had quickly found a more permanent place to stay, subletting a room from one of the emergency-room nurses.

The place wasn't nearly as great as the apartment she'd shared with John, but at least it was close enough to work that she could walk.

She'd done what she'd planned not to do. Returned to her old job at the emergency room.

She was right back in her old life.

Except more alone than she'd ever felt.

Which was crazy because she was surrounded by millions—literally—of people.

Cara worked her shift, grateful for the heavy workload because it kept her mind busy so she really didn't have time to dwell on anything other than the next patient.

"Um, Cara, the next guy requested you specifically," her nurse, and roommate, told her as she stepped out of the bay in which she'd just finished seeing a patient.

"What's wrong?"

"Hand laceration. Says he sliced it when getting out of his taxi."

"That's crazy. How'd he do that?"

The nurse shrugged. "Who knows? But he's a looker. Single, too. Apparently, he's just moved here and says he's hoping to find work soon."

"Probably an actor or an artist."

"I didn't ask. I was too busy staring into his eyes. I've never seen eyes that shade of brown before."

Cara's heart gave a jerk. How ridiculous that her nurse's description made her think of Sloan.

She left the nurses' station and crossed the room to the bay where the next patient waited. She pulled back the curtain and looked into eyes that were a particular coppery shade of brown she'd only ever seen on one person.

"Sloan."

God, she looked good. Too good. Maybe he had been wrong to come here. Wrong to think that Cara had felt the same about him as he had about her. Wrong to think she'd have missed him a fraction as much as he'd missed her.

He had missed her. Without Cara, life had lost its

luster. It had been as if he'd been living in a color-filled world and had suddenly been shot into black and white. Nothing glittered. Nothing shined. Nothing captured his interest.

His coworkers had known it. His patients had known it. His friends had known it.

Losing Preston had devastated him. Losing Cara had destroyed what was left.

Even more so when he'd realized, really realized, why he'd lost her. He'd been so wrapped up in what he wanted, a life in Bloomberg, that he hadn't let what Cara wanted ever register. Not really. He'd been no better than Preston, trying to emotionally manipulate her into doing what he wanted of her.

"What have you done to yourself?"

Her question had his gaze dropping to his hand. The nurse had given him a stack of gauze to keep pressed to his cut to slow the bleeding.

All professional, she squirted sanitizer into her hands, rubbed them together vigorously, then gloved up.

Without actually touching him, she lifted the stack of bloodstained gauze from his hand. She flinched at the jagged cut that ran along the frenulum of his thumb and pointer finger.

Her gaze lifted to his, full of confusion and something more. For all her professionalism, she couldn't hide that seeing him affected her.

"Why are you here?" Her voice was low, husky, accusing.

"I'd think that was obvious." He nodded toward his hand. "You promised to sew me up if I ever needed sutures."

Her gaze dropped back to the cut, then lifted to his.

"A trip to New York for simple sutures is a little pricey, don't you think?"

"There's nothing simple about what I need from you."

"Please tell me you didn't cut your hand intentionally."

"You know me better than that."

"No, I don't."

"Yes, you do."

She closed her eyes. "Okay, I know you well enough to know you wouldn't cut your hand on purpose, but no way are you going to convince me that it's a coincidence that you cut your hand and just happen to be in my emergency room."

"You're right. That isn't a coincidence. I came here with the sole intent of finding you."

"So I could suture you?"

"No, that happened when I got out of the taxi." He glanced at the cut again. "I'm not even a hundred percent sure how it happened. I was getting out of the taxi and brushed my hand across a plastic name plate on my suitcase that apparently had a very sharp edge."

Cara just stared at him. "Why are you in New York?"

"Because you are in New York." He glanced around the emergency-room bay. She'd pulled the curtain behind her, but there was no real privacy in the area. "Your shift should be about over. Sew me up, then let me take you to dinner and I'll tell you about the past six weeks."

"No."

"No, you won't sew me up?"

Without another word, she began prepping the wound for suturing. When she was ready to anesthetize him, she asked, "Are you allergic to anything?"

"Just penicillin."

"Noted." She injected the numbing agent into the area of the wound. The medication stung, but within seconds he could no longer feel anything she did.

She opened the suture kit, pulled out a needle with attached Ethilon and a pair of needle holders. As she pushed the needle through his skin and pulled the gaping flesh together, she sighed. "Sloan, this isn't fair."

"I'm the one at your mercy. What isn't fair?"

"I don't want you here."

Hearing her words hurt more than any physical wound that could be inflicted. If he'd believed her, her words would have created wounds no physician could heal.

"I'm banking on that not being true."

She wrapped the Ethilon around the tip of the needle holder repeatedly, tying knots then wrapping in the opposite direction to strengthen the overall effect of the suture's hold. She snipped the thread and quickly set about putting the next suture in.

"I don't understand why you're here. You've got everything you wanted from me already."

"You're wrong."

Her hands trembled ever so slightly, but she kept going, put in another perfect stitch and started a third one. "Before I left Bloomberg, I signed over my father's practice to you, his things. What more did you want?"

"His most prized possession."

"What's that?"

"You."

She tied off, snipped the thread on the third stitch and started a fourth. "You can't have me."

He watched her put in the fourth stitch, knew he was running out of time because five would close the wound completely. "Go to dinner with me."

"I've still got another—" she glanced up at the clock on the wall "—thirty to forty-five minutes before I get off work."

"I'll wait."

"What would be the point?"

"I flew to New York to see you."

"I didn't ask you here."

"You left without telling me you were leaving."

"There was nothing left to say."

"You sold me your father's practice for a dollar."

"It wasn't worth even that."

"You don't mean that."

"Quit telling me what I don't mean."

"You're right. I shouldn't do that."

"You shouldn't," she agreed.

"You left your father's things in the house."

"I didn't want them. I took the only things I wanted."

"Your mother's things?"

"Yes." She tied off the fifth suture, dropped the needle holder, needle and thread onto the sterile tray.

"You need to forgive him, Cara."

"I already have."

Cara had. It had taken her a while to work through her feelings toward her father. The reality was he was gone and she'd never be able to ask him why he'd chosen to do the things he had. But she had a good idea.

Preston had wanted her in Bloomberg. Wanted Sloan to be his son. Wanted his future grandchildren raised in Bloomberg. To him, manipulating their lives to where they would be thrown together had made perfect sense. He had been a man used to taking action, used to making things happen. No doubt her unwillingness to give him what he'd wanted had driven him crazy.

His manipulations had driven her there.

Or maybe it was that she'd actually fallen for Sloan that had driven her crazy.

She should have known better.

"This wasn't how I planned this, you know."

"That you had a plan at all is wrong."

"I should have flown to New York without a plan?"

"You shouldn't be in New York at all."

"Sure I should. I've moved here."

She stopped everything and stared at him. "What?"

"Go to dinner with me and I'll tell you everything."

She didn't want to go to dinner with Sloan. She'd actually told John she'd go to dinner with him and a couple of their friends at a nearby Irish pub. "I just can't, Sloan."

"Can't or won't?"

She hesitated. "I have other plans."

Something in the way she'd said it must have made him think she was seeing someone else, because his expression hardened. "You're seeing someone else already?"

"That's really none of your business."

"The hell it isn't."

She took a deep breath and waited. One. Two. Three.

"Dr. Conner, is everything okay here?" her nurse asked, popping her head behind the curtain.

"Everything is fine, Haley. I'm just finishing with Dr. Trenton."

"Doctor?" the nurse asked, looking impressed as she raked her gaze over Sloan. "What kind?"

"Family medicine. I've just moved here from out of state and actually have an interview here tomorrow with…" He gave the name of the human-resource director and the emergency-room director and gave the nurse a smile that was so amazing the heavens might have opened up and angels sung a tune. "You two are the only people I've met, but I'm really hoping to make friends here soon."

"Oh, wow. Nice to meet you." The woman smiled at him, took his bait, and did exactly what Cara didn't want her to do. "A bunch of us, Cara and I included, are going to O'Grady's, a couple of blocks from here. You want to join us?"

Sloan smiled at the woman, then at Cara. "That would be great."

"Seriously, you invited a total stranger to dinner with us?" Cara rounded on her nurse and roommate.

"Hello, are you blind? The man is gorgeous, intelligent, a doctor." Haley emphasized the words. "And will likely be our coworker very soon. Why wouldn't I invite him to dinner? If he's lucky, I'll invite him to more than that."

"No."

"No?" Her roommate's brows rose. "You calling dibs?"

"No." Cara put her fingers to her throbbing temple. "Yes." She rubbed the pounding. "No. Oh, I don't know. The man drives me crazy."

The woman's eyes rounded and her jaw dropped. "That's him, isn't it?"

"Him who?"

"The Southern doctor you dumped John for."

"I didn't dump John for another man. I left to go home to settle my father's estate. Sloan just worked at my father's practice. That's all."

Haley gave her a "duh" look. "Apparently not if the

man packed up his belongings and moved to New York to be near you."

"He didn't move to New York to be near me."

"Right." Haley looked convinced—not. "Keep telling yourself that."

"There's nothing between Sloan and me."

"Sure, because men quit their jobs and move to another state to follow a woman there when there's nothing between him and that woman." Haley leaned against the nurses' station and pinned Cara with her gaze. "Besides, it's not as if every one of us can't tell that something changed while you were down South, because you came back a different person."

"What do you mean?" she asked, knowing she sounded defensive.

"Because you rarely smile, never want to go out with us any more and look like you lost your best friend."

"My father died," Cara reminded her.

"True, and maybe that's all it is, but now that I've met Dr. Sexy from the South in there, I'd put my money on him being involved."

"You'd lose your money."

Her friend smiled and shook her head. "I don't think so."

Cara wanted to scream. How dare Sloan show up in her emergency room and cause all kinds of chaos? All kinds of speculation about what she'd been doing for the six months she'd been in Bloomberg?

Oh, how she despised him.

Only she didn't and no matter how many times she let the thought run through her mind, it wouldn't take hold.

Why was Sloan in New York? Had he really left the practice in Bloomberg and was moving here permanently? She didn't believe it. He loved Bloomberg. He'd never betray her father that way.

Did she really want to spend the rest of the evening under the watchful eyes of her friends, of John, with Sloan there?

She marched out to his examination bay, practically stomped over to where he sat, his suitcase on the floor beside the bed. "I will go with you, but just because I don't want my friends privy to the explanations you're going to give me as to why you're here."

"Okay," he agreed, as if he'd expected her to go along with what he wanted all along. "When can we go?"

"Dr. Koger is already here. Let me make sure everything is okay, grab my coat and then we'll head out. For a walk. Not dinner," she said, just to feel as if she had some control over the situation.

"Whatever you want."

"We've already established that this isn't about what I want, because I don't want you here."

For the first time he looked pensive. "Do you mean that? Do you really not want me here, Cara? Knowing that I've left Bloomberg and come to New York to find you and do my best to make things right between us, do you really want me to not be here?" He sighed, fatigue washing over his handsome features. "Because if that's the case, I'll go and I won't bother you again."

Cara's heart flip-flopped in her chest like a fish out of water. She wanted to tell him to leave. It's what she needed to do because he could only bring her pain.

But he was here.

He had left Bloomberg and was in New York.

Because he'd come to find her and make things right between them.

"I don't want you to go."

Relief washed over his features. "Thank you."

"For?"

"Being honest."

She narrowed her eyes at him. "I expect the same from you."

"That's easy. I miss you and want to be wherever you are. If that's New York, then I'll live in New York. Wherever you are, Cara, that's where I want to be."

"I've missed you, too." Darn it. Those were tears streaming down her face. She didn't want to cry. Not at all, but especially not in front of Sloan.

"Don't cry, Cara. I never want to hurt you. I'm so sorry that I did." He moved to her, stroked his good hand along her face. "Forgive me."

Cara squeezed her eyes shut. Forgive him. For what exactly? Her father had been the one to do the manipulating. Like herself, Sloan had been a pawn. A willing pawn but a pawn all the same.

"I can't bear to see you hurt." With that he bent and kissed her cheek, kissing her tears away.

Cara turned her head, causing her lips to meet his. She kissed him. She kissed him with all the angst swelling in her chest, with all the ache of not having seen him for six weeks. She kissed him with the passion that had rocked her whole world when she'd walked into the emergency bay and seen him sitting on the examining table.

"So good," he whispered against her mouth, kissing her deeper.

He was right. They were so good.

"Ahem." Haley cleared her throat. "I guess this means you're calling dibs after all?"

CHAPTER TWELVE

SLOAN PUT HIS suitcase down next to Cara's sofa and glanced around the tiny apartment she shared with her nurse. Tiny apartments. Busy streets. Tall buildings. No big open fields or clean air to breathe.

He'd just left Bloomberg and already he missed the town. He'd left a piece of himself when he'd packed his bag the night before and driven himself to the airport.

Six weeks he'd waited for Cara to come to her senses. Six weeks when he'd kept telling himself she would. Six weeks before it had sunk in that she was too much her father's daughter to admit she'd been wrong to leave him. She wouldn't be coming back and for him to try to manipulate her to was just as wrong as all that Preston had done. If he wanted Cara, he'd have to go to her. Would have to give up the life he wanted because being with her was more important than Bloomberg, his practice, the life he'd envisioned there.

Cara was that important.

He'd rather be with her anywhere than without her at the grandest place.

Now all he had to do was convince her of that because, despite their kiss, he knew she was nowhere close to letting him behind her walls.

"Maybe we should have gone with my friends after

all. There's not a lot to eat here," Cara said, turning from having hung their coats in the tiny closet just inside the front door.

"I didn't fly to New York because I wanted to eat, Cara."

"We're not doing that, either," she told him, obviously thinking he meant sex.

"I'd actually rather talk."

She walked across the room and sank onto the sofa. "Because you have a pattern of preferring talking to sex."

He grinned. "You're right, but this time I do."

She stared at him from where she sat. "So, talk."

He ran his finger over the bandage on his hand. "I had exactly what I wanted to say all figured out on the flight here."

"Then this should be easy."

"Nothing about you is easy, Cara."

"Probably not. I'm sorry."

"Don't be. It's one of the things I love about you."

She sucked in a deep breath. "Please, don't say that."

"That I love you?"

She nodded.

"Whether or not I say it doesn't change the truth. I'm in love with you. I have been for longer than you'd believe." He took a deep breath. "Actually, I fell in love with you before we'd even met."

"That doesn't make any sense."

"Probably not, but it's true. Your photos on Preston's office wall fascinated me. Your smile, the sparkle to your eyes, your daring spirit."

"Looking at my photo and wanting me is called lust, Sloan. Not love."

"True, but the way I felt about you went way beyond

lust." He met her gaze. "And Preston knew it. I'm not sure when he figured out that I was in love with you, but he knew."

"What makes you think that?"

"The way he talked about you, teased me about you, shared things about you that I don't believe he shared with anyone else. He let me see you through his eyes and, Cara, that's a beautiful and amazing view."

"I don't know what to say." She was floored by what he was saying. Was it even possible?

"You don't have to say anything. Just listen." He stood and paced across her apartment. "Cara, I'm not single because I want to be alone. I'm a man in love with you and no other woman would do. Will do."

Hope grew in Cara's chest. Could he be telling her the truth? Please, let him be telling her the truth.

"When Preston died I was devastated. Truly, the man was like a father to me, loved me like a son, but I believe that was because of you."

"What do you mean?"

"He knew how I felt, Cara. He knew and he encouraged my feelings, fed them, never let me forget you were out there, waiting for me. Only you weren't waiting for me, because you didn't know I existed outside the fact that your father had a new partner."

"I knew you existed. I detested you."

"I knew that, but I never could figure out why."

"Because you had my father's love and admiration without even trying to. I worked so hard to try to earn his love and respect and he just freely gave it to you. I was jealous. I…I think I still am."

"He loved you, Cara. He really did. He had a hell of a way of showing it, but he did love you."

"The will…" Her voice tapered off.

"Was a ridiculous attempt at playing matchmaker. It wasn't meant to hurt either of us. He just wanted to ensure we had the opportunity to work together, to get to know each other."

"How do you know that?"

He shrugged. "I just know."

"But Bloomberg…"

"Your father loved that town and its people, but he loved you more, Cara. In his mind, you were like him, not your mother. I can't tell you how many times I heard him say that you were just like him. He can't have been talking about looks because you're the mirror image of your mother. He thought if you saw Bloomberg through adult eyes, through eyes not clouded by the past, you'd love the town the way he did."

"I…" She almost said that she did, but did she? Or was she just getting choked up?

"I struggled with your father's requests of me from the beginning. Not because I didn't want you, not because I didn't want you to stay in Bloomberg, because I did. I do. I struggled because I was looking at everything through Preston's eyes and not yours."

"I don't understand."

"Preston believed you really loved Bloomberg and so deep down I believed that, too. Like him, I believed that if you just gave the town, the people, the clinic, a chance, you'd be like me and never want to leave."

"But you did leave."

He nodded. "I don't want to be somewhere you hate, Cara."

"I don't hate Bloomberg. I—"

"It doesn't matter. I've already found two doctors to work at the practice. Casey and another nurse practitioner I've hired are breaking them in. I'm not going back."

"Why not? You can't really be serious about moving to New York."

"I'm moving to wherever you are if you'll have me."

"Sloan…" She couldn't take any more. Not another moment. She stood and walked over to where he sat across from her. Dropping to her knees, she stared up at him. "I didn't want to like you."

"I know."

"Instead, I fell in love with you."

He dropped to the floor beside her, on his knees, cupping her face with his hands. "Tell me we have a chance."

Tears streaming down her cheeks, she nodded.

"I won't give up on us, Cara. I'll do whatever it takes to make this work."

She nodded again because words failed her.

"I want you to be just mine."

"I already am."

"I want us to do this right, to date each other without Preston between us. I want you to spend time with me because it's what you want, and when the time is right I want you to walk down the aisle to me and let me show the world how much I love you."

Her eyes widened. "You want to marry me?"

"This isn't a fling, Cara. I told you that long ago."

"But… Because of my father?"

"Because of you. Because of me. Because I love you more than life itself and I want to wake up beside you, go to sleep beside you every day for the rest of my life."

"I think I'd like that." Then she kissed him.

Neither of them heard the front door open, not until Cara's roommate cleared her throat.

"Fine," Haley intoned. "You get dibs on him, but I'm calling dibs on the bathroom first."

EPILOGUE

CARA ROLLED OVER in the bed and reached for her husband, only to find his spot empty. A slow smile stretched across her face. She knew exactly where he was.

Stretching first, she climbed out of bed, reached for her dressing gown and tiptoed out of her room. He wasn't where she first looked, but she soon found him sitting on the front porch, wearing only his pajama pants, rocking back and forth in the double rocker that had sat on the porch for as long as she could recall.

He smiled when he saw her. "We were trying to keep from waking you."

Her gaze traveled over the precious two-week-old snuggled against his chest, peaceful in the comforting reassurance of his father's heartbeat.

"I'd say you should have, but I must have needed the rest because I didn't hear you get up." She climbed into the chair next to him and reached out to touch their son because she couldn't resist the feel of his soft skin. "Hello, there, little guy. What have you and Daddy been up to out here?"

The baby looked at her from eyes that still partially crossed, yawned, then closed his eyes again.

"I've been telling him about how much I love his mom and how she grew up in this house and used to climb those trees over there and that someday he and I would build a tree house up there where those branches bow out."

"I always wanted a tree house in that tree," she mused, knowing the exact place he spoke of.

He took her hand. "I know. Your dad told me one night when we were sitting out here, talking. He told me if I ever had a kid to be sure to build them a tree house, because he'd never built yours."

"He told me he would," she recalled softly, trying not to let sadness seep in. She'd long ago forgiven her father for his unorthodox methods.

"That's what he said. That you two had bought the supplies and were going to build it together, but then he got called to the hospital and the tree house never got built."

"I remember."

Sloan squeezed her hand. "There will be times I get called to the hospital, Cara."

"There will be times I get called to the hospital, Sloan," she countered.

"But I promise you that Conner will have that tree house."

She knew what he was saying, that it wasn't the tree house he was really promising but that he would be there for their son in ways that she'd felt her father hadn't been for her.

"I know he will." She squeezed his hand back and laid her head against his shoulder, staring at their precious son. "He wasn't a bad father, Sloan."

"He was a good man, a great doctor and the best father he knew how to be at the time," Sloan agreed.

They'd discussed her father many times in the year

since Sloan had come to New York to be with her. Not that they'd stayed.

Her father had been right about many things. Sloan. Bloomberg. Her being a lot like him.

"I owe him everything," Sloan surprised her by saying.

"Why do you say that?"

"Because he brought you into the world and into my life."

Never had she felt so loved as she had the past year. Never had she felt she truly came first with another person until Sloan. He'd taught her so much about herself, about her father, her mother, who she was and who she wanted to be. The wife of a loving man. The mother of their son. A small-town doctor. A member of the community.

"I love you, Sloan."

"Love me forever and that'll be almost long enough."

* * * * *

MILLS & BOON®
Hardback – June 2015

ROMANCE

The Bride Fonseca Needs	Abby Green
Sheikh's Forbidden Conquest	Chantelle Shaw
Protecting the Desert Heir	Caitlin Crews
Seduced into the Greek's World	Dani Collins
Tempted by Her Billionaire Boss	Jennifer Hayward
Married for the Prince's Convenience	Maya Blake
The Sicilian's Surprise Wife	Tara Pammi
Russian's Ruthless Demand	Michelle Conder
His Unexpected Baby Bombshell	Soraya Lane
Falling for the Bridesmaid	Sophie Pembroke
A Millionaire for Cinderella	Barbara Wallace
From Paradise...to Pregnant!	Kandy Shepherd
Midwife...to Mum!	Sue MacKay
His Best Friend's Baby	Susan Carlisle
Italian Surgeon to the Stars	Melanie Milburne
Her Greek Doctor's Proposal	Robin Gianna
New York Doc to Blushing Bride	Janice Lynn
Still Married to Her Ex!	Lucy Clark
The Sheikh's Secret Heir	Kristi Gold
Carrying A King's Child	Katherine Garbera

MILLS & BOON®
Large Print – June 2015

ROMANCE

The Redemption of Darius Sterne	Carole Mortimer
The Sultan's Harem Bride	Annie West
Playing by the Greek's Rules	Sarah Morgan
Innocent in His Diamonds	Maya Blake
To Wear His Ring Again	Chantelle Shaw
The Man to Be Reckoned With	Tara Pammi
Claimed by the Sheikh	Rachael Thomas
Her Brooding Italian Boss	Susan Meier
The Heiress's Secret Baby	Jessica Gilmore
A Pregnancy, a Party & a Proposal	Teresa Carpenter
Best Friend to Wife and Mother?	Caroline Anderson

HISTORICAL

The Lost Gentleman	Margaret McPhee
Breaking the Rake's Rules	Bronwyn Scott
Secrets Behind Locked Doors	Laura Martin
Taming His Viking Woman	Michelle Styles
The Knight's Broken Promise	Nicole Locke

MEDICAL

Midwife's Christmas Proposal	Fiona McArthur
Midwife's Mistletoe Baby	Fiona McArthur
A Baby on Her Christmas List	Louisa George
A Family This Christmas	Sue MacKay
Falling for Dr December	Susanne Hampton
Snowbound with the Surgeon	Annie Claydon

MILLS & BOON®
Hardback – July 2015

ROMANCE

The Ruthless Greek's Return	Sharon Kendrick
Bound by the Billionaire's Baby	Cathy Williams
Married for Amari's Heir	Maisey Yates
A Taste of Sin	Maggie Cox
Sicilian's Shock Proposal	Carol Marinelli
Vows Made in Secret	Louise Fuller
The Sheikh's Wedding Contract	Andie Brock
Tycoon's Delicious Debt	Susanna Carr
A Bride for the Italian Boss	Susan Meier
The Millionaire's True Worth	Rebecca Winters
The Earl's Convenient Wife	Marion Lennox
Vettori's Damsel in Distress	Liz Fielding
Unlocking Her Surgeon's Heart	Fiona Lowe
Her Playboy's Secret	Tina Beckett
The Doctor She Left Behind	Scarlet Wilson
Taming Her Navy Doc	Amy Ruttan
A Promise...to a Proposal?	Kate Hardy
Her Family for Keeps	Molly Evans
Seduced by the Spare Heir	Andrea Laurence
A Royal Amnesia Scandal	Jules Bennett

MILLS & BOON®
Large Print – July 2015

ROMANCE

The Taming of Xander Sterne	Carole Mortimer
In the Brazilian's Debt	Susan Stephens
At the Count's Bidding	Caitlin Crews
The Sheikh's Sinful Seduction	Dani Collins
The Real Romero	Cathy Williams
His Defiant Desert Queen	Jane Porter
Prince Nadir's Secret Heir	Michelle Conder
The Renegade Billionaire	Rebecca Winters
The Playboy of Rome	Jennifer Faye
Reunited with Her Italian Ex	Lucy Gordon
Her Knight in the Outback	Nikki Logan

HISTORICAL

The Soldier's Dark Secret	Marguerite Kaye
Reunited with the Major	Anne Herries
The Rake to Rescue Her	Julia Justiss
Lord Gawain's Forbidden Mistress	Carol Townend
A Debt Paid in Marriage	Georgie Lee

MEDICAL

How to Find a Man in Five Dates	Tina Beckett
Breaking Her No-Dating Rule	Amalie Berlin
It Happened One Night Shift	Amy Andrews
Tamed by Her Army Doc's Touch	Lucy Ryder
A Child to Bind Them	Lucy Clark
The Baby That Changed Her Life	Louisa Heaton

MILLS & BOON®

Why shop at millsandboon.co.uk?

Each year, thousands of romance readers find their perfect read at millsandboon.co.uk. That's because we're passionate about bringing you the very best romantic fiction. Here are some of the advantages of shopping at www.millsandboon.co.uk:

* **Get new books first**—you'll be able to buy your favourite books one month before they hit the shops

* **Get exclusive discounts**—you'll also be able to buy our specially created monthly collections, with up to 50% off the RRP

* **Find your favourite authors**—latest news, interviews and new releases for all your favourite authors and series on our website, plus ideas for what to try next

* **Join in**—once you've bought your favourite books, don't forget to register with us to rate, review and join in the discussions

Visit **www.millsandboon.co.uk**
for all this and more today!